BLUE SAVAGE

BLUE SAVAGE

Earl Murray

Walker and Company
New York

W

First published in the United States of America in 1985 by the Walker Publishing Company, Inc.

Published simultaneously in Canada by John Wiley & Sons Canada, Limited, Rexdale, Ontario.

Library of Congress Cataloging in Publication Data

Murray, Earl.
  Blue savage.

  1. Oglala Indians—Fiction.   I. Title.
PS3563.U7657B58   1985   813'.54   85-10623
ISBN 0-8027-4048-0

Printed in the United States of America

Book Design by Teresa M. Carboni

10 9 8 7 6 5 4 3 2 1

For Lynette, who would have designed the lodges,
and Yvonne, who would have cared for the horses;
Tina and Pam, who would have danced to the music,
and Ryan, who would have carved beasts in the rocks.
I love them each one.

BLUE SAVAGE

Part One

*I came into this world, not chiefly to make this a good place to
live in, but to live in it, be it good or bad.*

H. D. Thoreau

CHAPTER 1

He walks among the Bad Face band of Oglala people, a man who has grown from a child lost on a desert to the threshold of greatness. It is said he will some day become a legend, as is the one called Red Cloud, who is now a leader among these people. They speak of him as strong and flashy in battle. His hair is the light gold of the morning sun on sandstone and his eyes the color of the evening sky. He is called Sun Hair and many are his honors.

But he walks now in a time when the Oglala people are to see a sudden and very swift change, as the knife that cuts to the bone renders the arm helpless from that moment onward. The drums of war no longer sound against the Crow or the Pawnee, but against the Wasicun, the white man—Sun Hair's true people. It has been a gradual thing, over the passing of many winters, that has now become serious. The Wasicun came with their white-topped wagons and their oxen and cattle, and horses of their own, and they did not care that they used all the grass and scared the game away from the streams and rivers. Isolated fighting brought the Bluecoats into these lands to protect the wagon people. There was more fighting. The fighting now continues.

The buffalo became less and less each year. The peoples of the Sioux, Cheyenne, and the Arapaho see each coming of the cold moons take more and more of the old and the very young. The anger and the sadness is everywhere. Something must be done to stop this, though the elders shake their heads and say that their dreams tell them to make peace, that it is better to try and live with the change.

The leaders of the many bands of the tribes will listen to their elders and talk to the leaders of the Bluecoats to try and make peace. Papers are drawn up by the Bluecoats to show these talks are important. It is the beginning of many promises . . .

3

They were a line of rolling blue against the brown and grey of the hills below the mountains. The snow had left with the winds of the season and the valley awaited the green of the warm moons. Sun Hair watched the blue line from the edge of the village while the council sat and talked among themselves. The young warriors had been told to put down their bows and leave their war paint within their lodges, for the Bluecoats had been asked to come this day. The rumor that Standing Bull would soon give up his adopted son had moved through the village like a swallow flitting along the cliffs. Sun Hair was to return to his true people.

Sun Hair hoped that it was a mistake. Wrong interpretations were common when talk between the Bluecoats and Indian people took place. Maybe the Bluecoats were coming only to see if he was happy among the Oglala, and to tell him he would be allowed to stay if he so wished. It should not matter, though, and there should be no circumstances under which he would be forced to leave the Bad Faces. He had always been honorable: he sang his songs of prayer morning and evening, as he had been taught as a boy; he loved the earth and sky, and gave homage to the four directions. Each time when the snow moons left and the grass began to appear, he danced with everyone to bring the buffalo. He was a good hunter and had also counted coup in war against both the Pawnee and the Crow. Many were the stories about him already. Many were those who praised him and told him they would follow him into battle. In just so very little time he would be a leader among them. Now, if this thing happened, this world would be gone.

The river was shallow and still lined with ice. Sun Hair watched the Bluecoats cross and come out near the horse herd below the village. With the Bluecoats were many horses without riders, signifying they were to be traded. Sun Hair's hope diminished with the low fog over the river and he became aware that the eyes of the villagers were now going back and forth from him to the Bluecoats. This was the last day of his life among them.

Sun Hair turned and walked back from the edge of the village, calling for his adopted father. His frustration at knowing what was to happen this day was mounting. He should have taken the rumor seriously and asked his adopted father if the whispered words were true. Outside the village, the Bluecoats were riding into formation and a horn was being sounded. Sun Hair found his adopted father and confronted him in anger.

"You told me I would always be your son. Now you sell me for horses."

"It is the decision of the council. Not my own."

"I have done nothing wrong. Why am I to be banished?"

Standing Bull waved his arm in a circle. "This is our land. It must always be this way. We do not want the *Wasicun* to come here, and we do not want the Bluecoats to protect them. The Bluecoats tell us if we give up our captives, we can live in peace and be bothered by them no more."

"I am not a captive and do not wish to leave."

"Your skin is white and you must go. That is the agreement."

The Bluecoats had entered the village and were talking with some of the war chiefs. Sun Hair's stomach began to tighten.

"I will run."

Standing Bull shrugged. "It is your decision, but you know you would be very foolish. You would be killed if you ever tried to return to this village. No other band would take you."

Sun Hair blinked hard. "It does not matter that you took me off the desert as a small boy lost and called me son? That I have brought you great honor as a warrior?"

"The council has decided."

"You could refuse the horses. If I must go, I will simply walk over to them."

"No. They must be made to pay. It is the way of things."

"I think you are greedy for horses."

Standing Bull's eyes grew hard. "You are indeed a *Wasicun*. You know nothing of respect."

Sun Hair struck quickly and without hesitation. Standing Bull fell back, his arms swinging like a bird shot in flight. Dog Soldiers ran over and Sun Hair struggled with them.

"No!" Standing Bull yelled. He came to his feet and spoke to the Dog Soldiers without looking at Sun Hair. "Do not harm him. We must not anger the Bluecoats now. He has put blood upon my mouth, but I will smile when he is gone and have many horses."

Helpless and alone, Sun Hair sat in a special lodge through the remainder of the day and the following night while the council smoked and ate and bartered with the Bluecoats and their scout, a man named Blanket Jim Bridger. Some called him Big Throat because of a growth on his neck. Sun Hair remembered him from his days as a child in the wagon of his parents as they traveled toward the gold fields of California. Bridger had been their guide.

When dawn came, Sun Hair was given a horse to ride and a plain blue jacket to wear. He was again a *Wasicun*. There were those who would miss him and those who would thank their spirit helpers for his leaving, but it was worth it to all to keep out the *Wasicun* and the Bluecoat soldiers who had come to protect them. The Oglala would see no more of the white-cloth wagons and the cattle that used the grass and water of the valley; there would be no more of these people with the white skin who thought of themselves as special and laughed when asked for presents of sugar, coffee, and tobacco in exchange for traveling through Indian lands. They knew nothing of this land and did not know how to treat it. Now that Sun Hair was gone, the Bluecoats promised this would happen no more.

They asked him if his name had been Harper and he nodded yes. They told him he was lucky, that other captives had died during their ordeal. He should be thankful to God in heaven for his good fortune, and to the United States government. He was told it was a special day for him and

that soon he would be able to dress right again, not like a savage. They told him many things while he passed the hills and mountains he had learned to call part of him, the creeks and rivers that had taken their place in his heart. After a time he refused to speak and closed his ears to all but the sounds of the earth and sky he was leaving.

Harper was now re-entering a culture he had been born into, but had never really known. His memories were only of his father telling his mother that he had a wagon in front of the cabin and that they were going to point it west toward a place called California. The trip had seemed endless and many had turned back, but Harper remembered his father's eyes and how he always kept looking straight ahead. On that burning desert they had run out of water but after a few days a man had brought skin bags filled with water to them. He would always remember how the people had fought over the water in those bags; how they had drunk greedily. Then he had watched them fall within minutes, doubled over with cramps, dying like so many birds over a poisoned carcass. His mother had fallen at his feet, his father close behind. When the scout came back with an arrow in his back and fell among them, Harper had been alone.

In his wandering, he had been found by Standing Bull and his war party of Oglala. They had traveled far to make war against and take horses from the Comanche. They had marveled at his stamina. He was taken among them as son to Standing Bull and came to be part of a culture he could not separate himself from. Within this culture all men were treated as equals since they had been given life by *Wakan' Tanka*, the Everywhere Spirit, the Maker of All Things. Intelligence, bravery, and good deeds were rewarded by added respect and a voice in the council, but no one considered himself to have absolute power. Instead, thanks was given *Wakan' Tanka* daily for the gift of life and a place in which to live upon the mother, Earth. Among the *Wasicun*, respect was measured by what was owned. They even called

the land theirs, which was a violation of faith in the True Way of Life. There was a constant struggle among them to achieve power over others, to feel better than those now considered beneath them. Many who were not considered worthy lashed out, only to find themselves imprisoned by steel bars and by men who would shoot to kill on order.

As he was growing up, Harper had learned much about the ways of the *Wasicun* from the old traders who trekked back and forth from their trading posts to the *Wasicun* villages, where dwellings were made permanent and the people did not move about to hunt. Harper had retained his ability to speak English by listening and talking to them when they wanted to know what it was like to live with Indians who had killed his parents. Harper had to keep telling them that his parents, and the rest of the emigrant party, had accidently poisoned themselves with bad water, but the traders still told the story of how he had fought the Indians and had been taken to become a warrior. This made for better campfire tales.

Taking him along with them to be sent out from these lands he loved, Harper said little to anyone. He learned a great deal from listening. The commander was Major Roland Deals, on special assignment to gather information about northern Indian tribes for the powerful white fathers far to the east. It was said he had many friends among these powerful men, who allowed him many liberties among the military. The Bluecoat soldiers talked about him whenever he could not hear them, and Harper learned how much this man was disliked.

He was called "Old Cornhead" by the soldiers because of his obsession with corn-on-the-cob and its annoying lack of availability. He had been sent out to headquarters from the famous Bluecoat post called Fort Laramie and his papers confirmed that he was not required to report to anyone, not even the post commander. He was not even to be listed on the roles, though he had the authority to assign soldiers to

details he would command, at his request. He was held in disdain by everyone, which failed to bother him in the least. In preference to a cavalry uniform of his rank, Deals wore fringed buckskins dyed a deep rust color and a campaign cap that someone said was an English safari helmet. He maintained a striking image and insisted those in his command remain loyal without question.

Deals paid no attention at all to Harper, and treated him as if he were only a piece of property. The first night out he had asked Harper if he could speak English. When Harper had remained silent, his remark to a ranking officer had been, "Once they become a savage, it is quite impossible to change them." This was in keeping with the unpredictable nature of the Bluecoat commanders, and a revelation in itself to Harper. Among the Indians, those who were looked up to for direction took responsibility for the safety and protection of those they led. Bad leaders were immediately voted out. Among the Bluecoats, those leaders who exercised respect and reason in their dealings with the Indian peoples were scorned and pushed aside by more aggressive types like Deals. It seemed a Bluecoat policy to be pushy and those good commanders who made promises on behalf of their people were told their words had no value. Honor among Bluecoats and their powerful *Wasicun* fathers in the East was not to be confused with authority.

During his ride with the Bluecoats from this land of his childhood and early youth, Harper tried to erase those memories that made him hurt most inside. The scars of the Sun Dance ceremony had been a source of great pride to him while among the Oglala. Now these Bluecoats only stared when they saw him with his robe open and wondered if he had been cut badly in battle. He could no longer let himself think of the day when he had first counted coup against an enemy and had brought a proud smile to the face of his adopted father. Harper could now see that same face frowning in anger at him. Maybe he should not have struck

Standing Bull, but betrayal is a thing that reaches deep into the heart and cuts with the edge of a hot blade. He touched a very small skin bag tied around his neck: his medicine bundle, filled with an elk's teeth, a buffalo stone, and the eyes and talons from his spirit helper, the red-tailed hawk that circles the skies. This was his power. He would keep it with him and he would always be strong. Though he would remember the pain of this day forever, he would remain strong.

"You are a stroke of very good fortune for me," Deals told Harper. "Of course you most likely cannot understand most of what I am telling you, but you are going to make me famous," he said to Harper as they rode into the fort to wild cheers.

Fort Laramie, the Bluecoat stronghold, had been built along the river of the same name, and was well known among the *Wasicun* who traveled into these lands, for all trails led there, the very sight of the fort making the *Wasicun* feel safe. The Indian peoples had once traded here in peace and Harper remembered that the Bad Faces had often camped at the fort to receive goods that came from the powerful white fathers in the East. Now he looked upon this place with a bitterness that settled deep within him.

All the Bluecoats watched while he was led toward the officers' quarters and placed beside a tub of warm water. Here they began to once again make him *Wasicun,* to make his outward appearance more closely resemble their own. With a dull pair of shears they cut his light blond hair to just above his collar, and made his wash the remnants of paint and clay from his body. They told him to discard the elkskin shirt and leggings, but this he would not do. He told them they had nothing better to give him; then when Deals began to speak, Harper pointed to his tailored buckskins but Deals waved the whole thing off. A wool suit with white shirt and tie remained untouched on a nearby bench.

Three other captives were present when Harper was led out to have a photograph taken. They had all been freed from separate bands of Sioux and had been at the fort hospital for nearly a week. Two of them were small girls who sat and stared, the third a woman who cried continuously and rocked back and forth. The Bluecoats saluted as Deals came over from the administration building and straightened his buckskin vest and safari helmet. He spoke with disgust at not seeing more captives and was told that these were all that remained throughout the various bands: the rest had either died or escaped.

Deals sent for the post surgeon, who came and sedated the woman. Harper was placed at the end of a wooden bench, the two staring girls seated next to him. The woman was arranged at the other end of the bench but kept falling off. When it finally became evident that she was unconscious, Deals ordered her taken back to the hospital. He would have to be satisfied with Harper and the two girls.

The photographer was finally ready and Deals took his place behind the bench, allowing the post commander to stand with him. They stuck their chests out and when the flash for the photograph exploded, one of the girls screamed and went into hysterics. Soon the surgeon was back and Deals ordered pictures now be taken with just himself, Harper, and one of the little girls.

When it was over, Deals strutted toward the administration building with the photographer, who worked for a large East Coast magazine and newspaper publisher. Harper was taken along to sign some papers that told how he had been saved from the Indians by Deals. He marked an X and smiled to himself when asked why he couldn't remember how to write. It hadn't occurred to them that maybe he had been too small when captured to have learned how in the first place. His silence made Deals feel very literate, but it bothered the other commanders, a few of whom Harper recognized. One in particular stared at him, remembering the filthy names

Harper had called him during a battle some years past. Deals told the post commanders that his report would be forthcoming and adjourned into a corner with the photographer.

"I have a written statement here from which you may take your story. It details the difficult circumstances we had to deal with in order to recover these captives. Make sure you emphasize that. Red Cloud would have killed us all if he thought he could get away with it. I put him in his place and our mission was a success."

No one noticed Harper as he got up and worked his way over to where the photographer had left the plates to dry. Harper picked them up and smashed them into the stone of the fireplace, then flung them across the room into a wall. The visiting stopped and the glaring began.

"I will not be made a fool of," Harper said, shocking the roomful of people. "Make pictures of yourselves, not of me."

"I must say," Deals commented, "you speak the language fluently."

"Before I had nothing to say. You all speak at once, as if what you say is important. They are all silly words. I had forgotten how silly they were."

One commander called the guards and Harper offered no resistance. He left with their rifles in his back.

"What if the word gets out that you put a returned captive in the guardhouse?" the photographer asked.

Deals thought for a time. He sensed the photographer conjuring up a fine story, one that would gain much more attention than those run-of-the-mill "Commander Saves the Day" type of things. With a wink at the photographer, he slapped his hands together and hurried after the guards. He ordered that Harper's confinement be changed from the guardhouse to the hospital.

"Be sure his hands and feet are secured to the bedposts. He is a very sick man and we can't have him hurting himself or someone else."

Harper then began to fight. Four guards wrestled with

him and finally one struck him with the butt of a rifle. The surgeon remarked that Harper's treatment more closely resembled that accorded a criminal than a rescued captive. The guards shackled the moaning Harper to the bed while outside the commander ushered the photographer to the officers' quarters where the drink of his choice was waiting. The photography could come later.

Late that night Harper finally realized his anger was not understood but abhorred by these people. Displays of temperament had served only to aggravate his problems and instill even more bitterness within him. He had been told by the Oglala he could no longer be one of them, and these people were not ready to accept him in their society. He was some sort of curiosity that had been brought in to break the boredom. Knowing he would be at this post only until arrangements could be made to send him East, Harper decided he would be far better off to go along with the circumstances until he was once again on his own.

His commitment to tolerance soon proved to be intolerable in itself. In exchange for his release from the hospital, he consented to another photography session; he hoped his bitterness expressed itself in the black and grey images that would find their way into newspapers and magazines. He was allowed to bunk in the cavalry barracks and immediately wished for the solitude of the hospital: the moans and occasional cries of the three delirious females in their beds seemed more in keeping with reality than the incessant bickering among the Bluecoats. Theirs was a world far different than his own and impossible to understand. Among the Oglala there was no list of rules, a man knew his own nature and supervised himself for the common good of the people. Morning sleep was not interrupted by a blast from a horn and meals were taken whenever the urge arose, not at three designated times during the day. These and other requirements were hard for Harper to grasp, the greatest of which was the daily routine he watched where

lines of Bluecoats marched endlessly in front of their leaders. To an Oglala warrior, it would have been very demeaning.

The days went by more slowly than any in his life since
being lost in the desert as a small boy. He kept hearing that
he would soon return East with a wagon train, but there were
few of those, since most were headed toward a new land
called Oregon. His life had been disrupted in a way he could
not understand, and he could find no way to deal with it. He
felt he could turn to his spirit helper, the red-tailed hawk,
who would bring power to him. He walked to the tops of
nearby hills in the mornings, in hopes of speaking with his
spirit helper, but there was always someone in a blue uniform close by to insure that he did not try to escape, which
frustrated him even more since the hawk would never come
down unless he was alone. His frustration mounted. There
was no use thinking of escape: the Oglala had given him to
the Bluecoats in good faith and his return to them would
only serve to cause anger and disdain. He realized he must
stay and await whatever lay ahead.

CHAPTER 2

The days grew ever warmer and the nights no longer held the cold breath of the snow moons. The grass raised its blades into the morning sun and birds sang nesting songs among the cottonwoods along the river. The women of the fort, mainly officers' wives, began to venture out from time to time with their shawls wrapped tightly against the incessant wind, wending their way along the paths to find the first blossoms of spring. They laughed with one another and it brought to Harper's mind visions of his childhood with his Irish mother. She loved flowers and their fragrance filled the kitchen each year at this time. Now this valley was filled with the color that comes with snowmelt and fresh rain, tiny bursts of beauty that overtook the land and made it a carpet of glory. Below the cottonwoods, the bright gold flowers of the wild currant and the ivory white of wild plum blossoms lined the banks and swales that reached back into the hills. Along the hills and valley floor were scattered colonies of wildflowers: the dancing scarlet of the delicate rooster-tails, the spinning yellow of the buttercup, and the fuzzy purple of the crocus-like windflower. They were fleeting, like the runner called Antelope who crossed these hills in grace and then was lost from sight. All these tiny flowers gave these women hope that this land was not forsaken by their God.

Among these hills in the evening, Harper began to see a solitary soldier, often sitting by himself. He played a small flute-like instrument common among the Irish troopers, usually referred to by them as a penny whistle. His music made Harper think even more of his mother, who sang many of the tunes the soldier played while doing her house-

15

hold work. Harper found one of his penny whistles on the ground atop a hill one day and took it to the soldier that evening.

"Mighty beholdin' to ye, me boy," the soldier thanked him in a heavy brogue. "I took to wonderin' where that might be." He laughed and opened his coat, which was lined inside with penny whistles of all sizes and shapes. "Can't say I missed it greatly."

Harper nodded. This man appeared to be as lost as he was. "You haven't been here that long, have you?" Harper asked him.

"Mickey O'Leary has never been anywhere very long, me boy. That's me trademark. But I ain't found a place yet I din't like."

O'Leary started another Irish jig. Red-grey hair poked out in all directions from under his worn blue cavalry cap, set off by green-brown eyes that danced like light on a pond. His uniform hung like a blanket on him and he had modified it by rolling up the trouser legs and sleeves. O'Leary finished the tune and stared at Harper.

"How is it you come to be more Injun than white man?"

"I prefer it."

"You can't hardly stomach it here, can ye?"

"White men do not have to live this way, any more than an Indian."

"There's no other way, lad. Not if you're white."

"Is that why you come out here into the hills then?" Harper asked. "To get away from it?"

O'Leary toyed with the penny whistle and pointed to a small pack of coyotes that had gathered nearby, sitting on their haunches with their ears erect and their tongues hanging out.

"They be music lovers, they be. That yeller one, why I saw him dancin' a jig last night." O'Leary laughed. Then he became serious. "You must think we're a sorry lot compared to them blood-drinkin' warriors you lived with."

"I have drunk as much blood as any of them."

"So I heard tell. You're still one of them, I'd say."

"I do not know who I am," Harper confessed. "The Oglala have sent me away and I do not wish to become a *Wasicun*. You are right when you say the Bluecoats are a sorry lot. Most of them have no more idea of what battle is than does a deer know how to fly. I can see now that the Bluecoats cannot possibly win the fighting against the Indian people."

O'Leary shrugged. "Can't say about that. But I sure ain't seen no action other than a trip through the hills on occasion. Fightin' is what I come out here for. It's in me blood, a part of me family, don't you see. They told me I'd be fightin' Injuns."

"What do you mean fight?" Harper asked. "Now that I and the other captives have been freed, there is to be no more fighting. There will be no more *Wasicun* wagons come into these hunting grounds."

O'Leary grunted. "That was Old Cornhead Deals who put that together for his own glory. That's all it be, nothin' else. He wants to get into politics back East. The big-assed son of a bitch. Hell, Washington don't know a thing about it."

"I don't understand," Harper said.

O'Leary got up and put his penny whistle back inside his coat. "You've got a lot to learn about the way things are, me boy. You're in with a different lot now."

A large band of Cheyenne, led by a chief named Black Kettle, made camp near the fort a few days later. They had heard all captives were to be released so had brought in two small naked girls, both exhausted but with their sanity. They were anxious to make peace with their white brothers; with the coming of the warm moons they had found buffalo and there would be a feast to show that their hearts were good. Harper watched as the warriors began to trade with the Bluecoats for robes and fur clothing, feeling secure in thinking that peace had finally come.

Nightfall came and the feasting continued. The Bluecoats showed little interest in the food, but instead spent their time giving brass buttons and cloth to the Cheyenne women in exchange for a trip into their lodges with them. The Cheyenne men would have objected ordinarily, but this was a time of sharing with their white brothers. Harper found it difficult to talk to any of them and all the women were told to avoid him. They could see in his eyes the desire to join them, to be among them when they left the following morning for their summer camps. He decided he would look for a horse he might steal. Knowing his intentions, he was followed constantly by warriors who gave wolf barks to those watching the herd. He was alone among many.

He had decided to return to the fort when he felt someone's eyes on him. He turned to see a woman across one of the campfires watching him, standing sideways with her arms crossed over her breasts. The firelight danced along her slim figure clad in an antelope dress. She had long, unbraided dark hair and raven eyes that flickered like jewels in the wall of a cave. He stood rigid, unable to move.

"It is you, Sun Hair," she said. Her tone was flat, without welcome or rejection. "I have heard the talk. When they spoke of how you looked and how you walked, I knew it could be no other."

Harper knew her well. Her name was Snow Fawn and she was blessed with beauty of a rare quality. Her blood was mixed, for she was the daughter of a fur trader and an Oglala woman. The fur trader had been killed in a fight with Pawnee and her mother had been taken as wife to an Oglala warrior shortly thereafter. It was a strange meeting for Harper, for he had once planned to marry this woman. Instead he had tried for the hand of a different woman, the daughter of an honored war chief named Man-Afraid-of-His-Horses, so he would be well thought of by the people. But this woman chose another and Snow Fawn's adopted father had in the meantime taken his family to live with

another band. Harper had scorned himself bitterly, for Snow Fawn was beautiful and would have been a far better wife. He had many times wished the chance to have her would come again, but already three winters had passed and it seemed their lives had separated forever—until tonight.

"Snow Fawn," he managed to say, "why are you among the Cheyenne?"

"I no longer live with my mother and adopted father. My husband is Cheyenne."

"Your husband?"

"Did you think I would never marry? Not long after we left the Bad Face band, I became wife to a Cheyenne warrior called Elk-Dancing-at-Night. It is strange that you should ask, or even care. You did not wish to have me as your wife. Did you know I left carrying your child?"

Harper stared. Finally, he asked, "Why did you not tell me this?"

"You were to busy chasing the daughter of Man-Afraid-of-His-Horses. You avoided me and I could not get near you. That is why you never learned about your child. He is called Fox Boy."

Harper watched while she went into a nearby lodge and returned with a small boy. Snow Fawn stood next to Harper and the firelight shown on a small head of brown-blond hair.

"He has passed two winters now," Snow Fawn said. "Do you wish to hold him?"

Harper took his son and looked into small dark eyes that saw him as a stranger. The boy had the jutting Harper jaw and a delicate nose like his own mother's. Fox Boy. His young muscles were tense and showed strength as he wiggled in Harper's arms. His skin was a fine copper, smooth and warm, like his mother's. Harper suddenly felt bonded to the child. His blood was in Fox Boy and this realization gripped him stronger than any sensation he had ever known. The boy began to whine and Snow Fawn took him back.

"You could have held him every day," she said to Harper.

"You could have shown him the ways of hunting and scouting for enemies. He would have called you Father and boasted of your coups in battle. But now he will not. He will never know who you are, for he will have a different father to care for his needs."

Fox Boy was staring at Harper from his mother's arms. Snow Fawn's eyes were mixed with hurt and anger.

"We could not have been married," Harper said. "Your father did not like me because of my blood."

"My father did not like you because you were not truthful with me. You played the love flute for me and I came out to meet you. Then you did not bring presents to him in exchange for me, but instead began to court another. My adopted father would not have asked for much. He thought highly of you, since you were quite young to have counted coup against two enemies. He thought you would some day repay him many times over. He was not angered by the disgrace, only saddened."

"They would have made me leave you anyway," Harper rationalized. "I was once a captive. All those who are *Wasicun* are now to be given up."

Snow Fawn shook her head. "No. All those who have taken a wife or who have become a wife are to remain with their families. They will be hidden and they will be kept secret. The Bluecoats will never know about them."

Harper's mouth dropped. Commanders from the fort had begun to make their way through the village, threatening the guardhouse to anyone not in their quarters within the hour.

"Are you happy?" Harper asked her.

Snow Fawn blinked and turned her face from him. "It is said that you will return to the land of the *Wasicun*, far away where Sun rises each day. I will leave you now, so that you can prepare for your journey." She turned back to him and the tears glistened on her face. "I hope you will be happy, Sun Hair, when you reach the *Wasicun* lands. I will ask *Wakan' Tanka*, the Everywhere Spirit, to watch over you."

Harper watched her disappear into the lodge with Fox Boy. He thought of following her, but warriors were watching. One of them might be Elk-Dancing-at-Night. Instead he turned and made his way out of the camp toward the fort, through a darkness far blacker than any he had ever before known.

The days now seemed strange for Harper: a part of his life had returned in a manner he had not dreamed possible. Though he had not forgotten his young woman whom he had once become intimate with, he had never expected this.

Black Kettle's band of Cheyenne stayed for the remainder of the week, but Harper resisted his temptations to once again see Snow Fawn. Another band of Cheyenne, under a warrior named White Antelope, had joined the encampment and there were good feelings among them for the Bluecoats. Harper could ill afford to disrupt these growing feelings of good will by angering Snow Fawn's husband. Harper had to be satisfied with watching White Antelope from the hills overlooking the fort and wishing he had made the right decision those three winters past. He now wished he had never seen Snow Fawn or the boy; it only made him more confused and helpless.

The morning after the Cheyenne left, Harper walked out from the fort and into the valley, which seemed empty. The wind made its continual crying sounds through the cottonwoods along the river, their leaves now unfurled from the buds into wide blades of olive green that turned and twisted and glistened in the light as the breezes danced among the branches. Somewhere along the banks of the river the little bird called killdeer made its high-pitched call that always sounded like it was lonely.

In the empty camp were discarded cooking pots and forgotten blankets and robes. When morning drills were finished this bottom land would be swarming with Bluecoat soldiers searching for souvenirs to write home about. To

them the Indian peoples were a source of fascination and they spent much of their time talking among themselves about how open and trusting these people were, like so many children to whom you could say anything and have them believe it.

The days watching the Cheyenne had been an education for Harper. It became plain to him that their condition was already serious and that they were worse off than any of the northern tribes. The *Wasicun* had filled their lands with roads and square-shaped lodges made by stacking logs of cottonwood or pine. The buffalo had mostly been killed or driven away from the valleys and hunting had become very bad. It was evident even as these people came to the fort to talk of a lasting peace that their children suffered from hunger and disease. And the very old could not even be seen among them.

The *Wasicun* came to find new lands but had found a special yellow metal that made them crazy and brought hoards of wagons streaming into the lands to the south against the mountains. It was said they dug holes in the hills and sat in the freezing water of mountain streams for long periods of time to try and find it. They traded it for goods and it was a means of wealth, as horses and war honors were to the Indian. Now both the Cheyenne and Arapaho tribes were being pushed aside to make room for more *Wasicun*. As all this began to happen, the peoples of the Cheyenne and Arapaho had divided into northern and southern groups. Black Kettle and White Antelope had wished to stay south. It bothered Harper knowing that Snow Fawn and Fox Boy were going back down to a place where the *Wasicun* had become many and where there were sure to be more bad times. The favorite place of the southern branch of the Cheyenne now was along the Little Dried River—a place called Sand Creek.

Only days after the Cheyennes' departure, freight wagons

appeared on the horizon to the east. With them were many of the white-cloth wagons. These emigrant wagons were most certainly bound west.

O'Leary's comment about trying to understand that there would never be peace was foremost in Harper's mind now. He showed his frustration by stabbing the ground with a sharp stick, for he was every bit as trapped as he had ever been. The Bad Faces were no longer his people and even if he tried to explain to them that the words of the Bluecoat leaders had been hollow, they would not believe it until it was too late. They would not understand this until they were starving because the buffalo were gone. They had given their word to the Bluecoats and would accept no change in their agreement.

With the freight wagons came the soldiers' pay and mail from the East. The parade ground was amass with yelling men hugging one another and jumping up and down. Soon card games started up in all the barracks and a number of soldiers began dancing to tunes on fiddles and banjos. The officers brought their wives out and by the middle of the afternoon the new spring grass where the soldiers drilled was visibly worn from the stomping and twisting of a thousand boot heels.

Harper had been watching from the doorway of the sutler's store. Deals saw him and straightened his safari hat and brushed down his tailored buckskin suit. He held a newspaper open for Harper and pointed to a large photo with many lines of print surrounding it. The photo showed Harper on the wooden bench with Deals standing directly behind and to one side. In Deals's hand was a cavalry sabre, which he held upward, pressed tightly against the front of his right shoulder. This photo had come from the second session, where the two small girls and the woman had been omitted so that Deals could tell a story about how a white warrior among the Sioux had been brought back to civilization. Deals read Harper a part of the article, which stated

that Harper was now doing well for himself somewhere in the East and that Deals had been brought up for a medal of honor.

"An excellent story," Deals commented to Harper. "I must say, the photograph would have been much better if you could have managed to smile, even just a bit." He folded the paper and placed it under his arm. His eyes appeared indifferent. "It is amazing how you insist on retaining your savage traits."

As Deals turned, Harper quickly asked, "Could I see the picture again?"

Deals studied him. "You don't intend to ask for it, do you?"

"I just want to see it again."

Deals hesitated an instant, then unfolded the paper and exposed the story page. Quickly and with accuracy, Harper spit directly on the image of Deals in the picture and walked out onto the parade ground. When Deals finally recovered, he came out onto the parade ground trembling with rage. He found Harper standing in the midst of the frolicking, dancing hoards of men and women. Harper turned to face Deals, hoping he would cause an incident, but Deals realized there was no one who would likely care in the least about spittle on his picture. The chances were greater they would applaud it.

Deals slurred through his teeth at Harper, "You are indeed a savage. God help you if you ever find yourself in this army."

Harper watched him march out of the crowd of dancers, his arms rigid at his sides, the paper folded tightly, crushed in the clasp of one hand. He made his way off the parade ground and into the officers' quarters, never once looking back at Harper.

During the following week, passengers for an eastbound emigrant train began to assemble at Fort Laramie. As more and more came, Harper watched them stand around the parade ground and watch the soldiers drill. Rarely did they

laugh or even smile. They just wanted to know when the soldiers would be ready to escort them back to civilization. Mostly stragglers from various westbound trains, they had decided that living in untamed land wasn't worth the trouble or, in the majority of cases, the pain. Many had lost children to weather or disease in a land far different from what they had envisioned. Others had simply lost their courage: stories about child-stealing Indians kept mothers awake nights, reaching through the darkness for small lumps in nearby blankets. For one reason or another, they wanted to go back.

This type of thing was not a priority in the eyes of the fort commanders, though they were under orders to protect emigrants regardless of their direction. A "failed train" was looked down on by everyone in ranks. When a cavalry detachment to escort the train was finally selected, the departure of the wagons was met without fanfare. No one among either the emigrants or the army paid much attention to Harper now. He didn't belong to anyone's organization and there was little reason to think that anything he did from here on would matter much to anybody. The emigrants had heard of his life with the Sioux and seemed more afraid of him than anything else. They watched him and then turned their faces when he made eye contact. He ate alone and rode by himself when the wagons were moving. At night he listened to the laughing soldiers and watched them point at the emigrant women, while the emigrants talked and pointed at him.

While they traveled, Harper noticed signs that they were being watched and followed. He told no one and made decisions for himself based on what he saw. They were Cheyenne and Sioux, likely Oglala. Why they watched the train was a mystery: these wagons were leaving their hunting grounds, never again to come into these lands. Why would these warriors spend their time at this? From the sign he could tell that they were mixed Cheyenne and Sioux but not how many there were.

Finally he realized that these warriors were following

because of him. They played tricks with their signs to confuse him, knowing he could read them. He saw buffalo skulls painted in a sign, which meant that a battle would take place at a certain point along the river. But it did not happen. He saw stones layered upon the hills foretelling an upcoming council, but no one ever appeared on the hilltops making sign for talk. It was all a game, and he knew it bothered them that he showed no concern and did not tell anyone. He would wait for their move.

At a place called Chimney Rock, a messenger from Fort Laramie came into camp one evening. Before dawn the entire escort detachment was headed back to Fort Laramie, deaf to the loud protests of all the men and the crying of all the women. The messenger had brought news that an emigrant train going north from the fort had been attacked by Sioux and that there had been no survivors. Priority now lay with punishing the Sioux.

The wagons remained in a circle, the men discussing what they would do while the dust from the vanished escort column clouded the morning air. Harper stood atop a wagon seat, his eyes searching the hills along the river, reading what sign he could. He hoped the party of Cheyenne and Sioux that had been following the wagons would now decide to go after the soldiers. But the sign read that the wagon people would sing their death songs very soon.

There came a laugh from the wagon just ahead of him and the face of Mickey O'Leary appeared, framed by the white canvas of the wagon.

"How about a little tune before breakfast?" O'Leary suggested. He jumped from the wagon and began to play a jig on one of his penny whistles. He danced and turned and played while everyone stared. Some of the children began to laugh, but their mothers kept them at arm's length. The men finally asked him what was going on and he laughed and asked them if they didn't know Irish music when they heard it. Then he came over to Harper and grinned up at him.

"I found me way out of that damned outfit, I did. I'm as free as a bird, I am." He climbed up next to Harper.

"I thought you wanted to fight," Harper said.

"I been watchin' the sky at that post, is all I been doin'," O'Leary said. "That and ruinin' me stomach on stale bread and tainted pork. I don't rightly call that a real battle. What you lookin' at out in them hills?" He began to toy nervously with the penny whistle.

"The messenger said you would be fighting once you found the war party that attacked the *Wasicun* wagons," Harper said, ignoring the question.

O'Leary shrugged. "I've heard that before. I figure to go back to where a real war is set to go off. Talk is that the South aims to pull out of the Union. I figure that will call for some shootin' back and forth."

"I have told nobody up to now," Harper said to O'Leary, "but there is a war party watching us."

O'Leary nearly dropped his whistle. His eyes turned to the hills outside of camp and his mouth began to twitch. "You'd be foolin' me now, wouldn't you?"

"No. They have been traveling in the hills beside us ever since we left the fort."

O'Leary became more nervous. "Why didn't they attack before now? Why haven't we seen them?"

"That is the way of an Indian warrior," Harper explained. "When his medicine is good, then he will fight."

"Sweet Jesus!" O'Leary blurted, making the sign of the cross. He turned to Harper. "Do you figure they'll come down on us."

"I can't say," Harper answered. "The sign has been strange all the way. But I think they will, now that your Bluecoat friends have gone. Is that the way all *Wasicun* protect their brothers?"

"Wagon folk and soldiers don't mix," O'Leary said. "But I didn't figure on this, or else I would have gone back with the others. The numbers here just ain't fair!"

CHAPTER 3

For three days the wagons rolled toward a distant place called Fort Kearney. The detachment from Fort Laramie was to have accompanied them to the South Platte River, where a Fort Kearney detachment would escort them on to the edge of the Oregon Trail. Though neither Harper nor O'Leary had mentioned anything about Indians, it seemed everyone in the train was aware of the eyes that continually watched them. Harper could not understand why the war party had made no appearance, nor why the sign stopped all of a sudden.

The emigrants had looked curiously at Harper the day the cavalry had left them. Suddenly he had become their only link to survival. Those who had looked away from him before begged for his leadership now. Doctors and lawyers, farmers and storekeepers alike, who had shunned him before because he was not one of them, now wanted his services. Harper wondered how they could remain sane since they changed their minds all the time, and he wondered how it would be after they reached Fort Kearney.

Harper gave orders that nobody liked. He made them dump all personal possessions with the exception of their rifles and one change of clothes apiece. The goods were consolidated into half the wagons and those remaining burned and left behind. Mules and cattle and oxen were turned loose, only the strongest were kept to pull the remaining wagons. Everyone but the smallest children walked so that the wagons might move faster and farther each day. Food was not taken at midday, but only in the morning and late evening, after the wagons were stopped for the night.

29

None of them spoke to Harper unless asked a question, for they began to hate him. But none of them rebelled, since something in his eyes told them their lives would be worthless without him.

Behind Harper the wagon train moved into a rhythm, exhausting but continual. There was no time to worry about aches and pains and Indians, or the past they were now leaving behind. Their bickering and quarreling stopped and they used what strength was left at the end of each day to care for themselves and their children. Harper rode in front each day with O'Leary, listening to stories of fights that never happened and women he never knew. O'Leary was a history book: he talked with knowledge about the Irish and their heritage of war over the centuries. It was a fact that the Celts would never give up their way of life, that they had always repelled all invasions or had sent themselves to a sure death rather than embrace slavery. O'Leary asked Harper if these warlike Indians were of the same nature and Harper said they were.

"I figure you know me pretty good by now," O'Leary said to Harper as they got ready to stop for the night. "Maybe I should say that I said more Hail Marys on patrol than any shots I ever fired at Injuns."

Harper ordered the wagons to circle. For some unknown reason the war party had left and now it would be good to rest. Women and children eased down from the wagons to stretch cramped legs and relieve themselves in the cover of the trees along the river. Finally Harper and O'Leary got down off their horses and led them to the river to drink.

"Do you worry about what I think of you?" Harper asked O'Leary.

"I'm a soldier, according to this blue uniform," O'Leary answered. "I'd hate for people to think I never drew down on an Injun. Especially at my age."

Harper held his horse's nose, to keep the animal from gulping the water. "There are men among the Oglala that

have white hair and a lot of wrinkles who have never shot a bow in their life, or never went on a war party to steal horses or kill an enemy. Nobody thinks less of them. They are what they are."

"You're spoofin' me, Harper."

"It is the truth. There are many of them. Some of them are considered chiefs. Peace chiefs."

O'Leary straightened his shoulders and pulled his horse's nose out of the water. "Well, I'll be go-to-hell. Maybe I just found my callin' after all."

Harper went to the top of a hill just before sundown to look for sign. On his way up he found one of O'Leary's penny whistles on the ground. He studied its small linear design, fingering the notched holes in the narrow wooden stem. It recalled the love flutes common among the Indian peoples, suddenly bringing Snow Fawn to mind. He longed for her now like never before. He had played the love flute for her often, and now it seemed he was drawn back in time.

Light from the scattered fires in the circle of wagons below danced in the late day and the white of the wagon covers turned crimson as the sun disappeared. Harper realized he had been blocking O'Leary's music from his mind; he had been listening, but had been fighting the memories of his own music and what it had meant to Snow Fawn. He had tried to relate O'Leary's music to his mother, whose Irish voice had once flowed with the tunes so common from O'Leary. But since coming to the Oglala Harper had learned to play a love flute himself, and this night carried him back to the Bad Face village.

He sat down and began to play Snow Fawn's favorite song. His fingers moved deftly as his lips pushed air through the wooden tube and the notes drifted out into the early night, a slow melodic tune in the tradition of the Oglala and other Plains Indians. He had made it up for her, stylistically beautiful, haunting and vibrant in expression. It brought

nighthawks in and now an owl would sweep low and glide back out again into the vast black sky. In the circle of wagons, the people all turned their heads and began to gather together, pointing up and talking. No one was afraid and all knew who was making this music. It served to deepen their curiosity about this white Indian named Harper.

O'Leary walked up the hill and stood at a distance for a time until Harper had finished the tune. He came over next to Harper and sat down.

"I tell you, me boy, you'd bring tears to the eyes of a hangman."

Harper held the whistle out for O'Leary to take. "I should have asked you before I played it."

"Nonsense!" O'Leary said gruffly. "It's yours. I've got plenty more where that comes from, you know. How did you learn to play like that?"

Harper shrugged. "I learned as a boy with the Bad Faces."

O'Leary shook his head. "I've played all me life and I've heard them all, but there's the splendor of God Himself in what you can do. I'll leave the playin' to you from now on."

"No," Harper said. "I do not want you to stop playing now. Why would you do that?"

"I figured I was good," O'Leary said, "but I ain't nowhere near as good as you, me boy."

"That is not right," Harper told him. "The Everywhere Spirit, the Great One, did not put us here to stand back from one another. Instead we must learn and be touched by what we see and hear. We are to rejoice in one another. Each of us has qualities others wish to possess, but we must all understand those qualities cannot be given to everyone. It would be foolish for you to quit playing around me. I do not think little of you."

"You can't see it my way," O'Leary tried to explain. "I could practice for the rest of me life all day, each day, and never play like that."

"But what you do play makes you feel good."

"Yes."

"Then don't think of me as better than you. Think of me as different than you."

O'Leary thought a while. "I 'spect you're right, at that."

"You give me pleasure with your music," Harper went on. "There is one song my mother sang when she washed clothes, called 'The Last Rose of Summer'."

O'Leary laughed. "Yes, yes, me mother sang it all the day long. I think of her a lot in this lonely country."

"The country is not lonely," Harper said quickly. "If you will let it, the country will be your friend. There is consolation in a blade of grass. Trees and flowers will talk to you, if you will listen. Even the wind is a song."

"I've not met a man like you before," O'Leary said. "You're rock on the outside, but underneath your heart is down from a wee duckling. Maybe things will get better for you when we get back to the settlements."

"I'm going to have a hard time of it. Nothing is the same in this world. I can see now there are good people with white skin, but it is so very hard for them to be themselves. They believe they must be someone else to be accepted by others. This is strange to me."

Harper toyed with the penny whistle, staring down at the people in the ring of wagons. They were shouting and waving for him to come down.

"You've touched them all, me boy," said O'Leary. "Every last one."

"I must play alone," Harper said. "This night I must play alone."

O'Leary nodded. "I might be out of place in sayin' this, but I'd bet you was makin' music to a woman."

"I must stay on the hill."

O'Leary rose to his feet and walked down the hill among the wagons. The people all gathered around him and

Harper could see him explaining to them that the white Indian wanted to be alone. Some wandered off to bed while others stood and stared up the hill into the darkness to where this strange mystical music carried out into the night. They wondered at this man who seemed to have no feeling, yet carried within him the gift of musical talent. It seemed more than mere talent, this display of inner feeling that rose into the night and held them spellbound. This man was far stranger to them now than ever before.

Later that night Harper realized his music was not going to bring Snow Fawn back and he smashed the penny whistle. He reached for his medicine bundle and in his loneliness could get no feeling of power from it. He had worn it religiously, even after being taken from the Bad Faces to the Bluecoat post at Fort Laramie, and now had to fight the feeling that its powers had left. He could not afford to do this, for his personal medicine was contained in that small skin bag and to lose confidence in it could easily bring death. This he had learned as a child and the thought of it began to haunt him. He must be strong, he told himself; he must realize Snow Fawn would never again be a part of his life and he must look ahead. The red-tailed hawk would come in time, when the bird was ready to speak to him. Time. It could be measured quickly, or ever so slowly. It was best to allow life to carry it quickly.

The next afternoon Harper circled the wagons when a huge herd of buffalo could be seen blocking the trail ahead. They were migrating north into the cooler grasslands for the duration of the warm moons. They were black against the green waves of grass for as far as the eye could see. At first the wagon people were fascinated but in time grew bored and made suggestions to Harper about going through them. Harper told the people that the only thing they could do was wait for the herd to pass, which would likely be within a day or two. And there was to be absolutely no hunting: even

though the war party had left, Harper wanted no reasons for an attack should they return.

Fires were placed outside the circle of wagons to keep the herd at a distance. Should any buffalo begin rubbing against the wagons or become angered with the mules and oxen, a great deal of damage and possible loss of human life could result. No chances were to be taken.

That evening Harper said his prayers atop a small hill above the river and thought of the many times he had given thanks to *Wakan' Tanka* for the buffalo. The dark coats of the cows and bulls were brown in the late afternoon sun. The tawny coats of the newborn calves glowed like spun gold as they romped and played along the edge of the herd, running and kicking and butting heads. He had reached the last of this wild land and it was as if it had a final goodbye to say, a last glimpse of an early life to be left far behind, yet it would never really leave, but linger within like the smell of pine in an evening forest. A feeling so strong could never pass, but grow with each day and push its way deeper into the mind.

O'Leary made his way up to the top of the hill and said he hoped he wasn't interrupting anything. Harper had finished his prayers and was just watching the buffalo. He told O'Leary he would enjoy the company.

"Life ain't nothin' I'll ever be able to figure out, me boy," O'Leary commented. "The last time I felt as good as the day I left the damned army was the day I joined it." He pulled a small black book from his jacket pocket and began to write in it. After a time he looked up at Harper again. "I usually write off by meself. Up to now I didn't care to let anyone even know I wrote down me thoughts."

"How long have you been keeping a diary?" Harper asked.

"Oh, you keep a diary, do ye?"

"My mother kept one. I should have tried to find it that day they all poisoned themselves on that water. I guess I was too small to care."

"Me own mother kept one as well," O'Leary laughed. "God

bless her, she taught me to read and write." He talked to himself for a time while he wrote on the small unlined pages. Then he shoved it in front of Harper to read.

"I wasn't old enough to learn," Harper said. "The Oglala tell their stories in pictures."

"Nothin' to be ashamed of," O'Leary assured him.

"I'm not," Harper said.

"How good are you at listenin' then?" O'Leary asked.

"I would be happy to listen," Harper nodded.

O'Leary flipped through the pages. "I'll start the first night I met ye, back at Laramie when ye found me penny whistle."

Harper listened while O'Leary read from the small black book:

18th April 1859
Met whit Indin named Harper today. Fine fellow.
He wont sculp me. Plan to stay on his goode side.
Windy. Butiful sunset.

O'Leary tipped his blue cap and referred to the passage about losing his scalp. "I guess I give meself a bit more credit than I deserve." He pointed to the thinning patch of red-grey hair atop his head. "I ain't got enough to make it pay."

"Why are you afraid to die?" Harper asked.

"It ain't natural not to be."

"To a warrior it is an honor. To the Irish it is an honor."

"For the right cause it is an honor," O'Leary said emphatically. "The truth is I can't get meself to fight these Injun people out here. They be too much like me own folk back home. They'd sooner die than pull a yoke for someone else. I figure to be more with these Injuns than against them. You can rightly see that, can't ye?"

Harper nodded. He looked into the western sun, far out to where the distant mountains were slim blue humps with a jagged middle that was Laramie Peak. Far north were the ragged Bighorns where cool nights were spent thinking of

Snow Fawn. Even when he had thought he wanted the daughter of Man-Afraid-of-His-Horses he had dwelt on Snow Fawn's tender touch of love. She had once thought a great deal of him, pointing out to all how the buffalo came to him so that he could make meat and how enemy warriors ran from him in fear. His mistake in leaving her had been a great one and it seemed even more harsh now that the mountains were dissolving with distance. This woman and his times with her were now gone and the land of the *Wasicun* could never be as sweet, the touch of another woman never so pure.

"I can see them green hills across the creek," O'Leary was saying. He had turned and was facing eastward, his knees drawn up under his chin, as a boy sits on the bank while he waits for a fish to bite. "It's home I see, it's home! And I be there now with a line in the water and a string o' big fish on the bank beside me. She's singin', me mother. Can't you hear her? So sweet in the air beside her washin'. And me father be fittin' blocks o' peat into the shanty to make it bigger, for baby Colleen has come. The crops be standin' ready in the fields, but it's the baby's laugh he's got in his heart. God bless him! They be gone now. They all be gone. Bless them, God bless them all. How I miss them."

Harper was again facing westward and on the face of the scarlet setting sun were the eyes of a small boy who now called him Father. On the wind was Snow Fawn's voice calling him back, informing him that there was no Elk-Dancing-at-Night and that she had never married. He saw Fox Boy growing, riding his pony at full speed, his small knees locked against the pony's ribs, a bow and arrow in his short fingers. He stood with Snow Fawn, proud, happy, as Fox Boy walked into the village weak and hungry but blessed with honor at having completed his vision quest, a dream holding all who heard it spellbound. Then the sun was gone and a wisp of wind took the images away from Harper and scattered them across the waving grasses of these plains, drenched in the red glory of twilight.

O'Leary was talking again. "This is all too much like back home, don't you see. These redmen be poor folks and they got nothin' but their homes and each other. They want nothin' else, I can see, just as it was with us. We weren't about to bow to the crown of England and the blokes knew they'd have to kill us all first. So they stopped fightin' us, you see, but they took and took and took until there was nothin' left." O'Leary was staring down at the buffalo as he spoke, watching them line the river for miles, massive black shapes in the lost light that sloshed in the shallows and bawled for lost calves. "They gave us whiskey, but we had no food. The blight came and the potatoes rotted in the fields. Soon we had nothin' but the rags we was wearin' and each other. We watched them die, brother Barney and me, Mother and Father and wee Colleen, and then we got on a boat to come across and I watched Barney take sick. He asked me to help him and I couldn't, and they dropped him over into that big ocean, God rest his soul." O'Leary was staring out into the last thin glimmer of twilight along a distant stretch of the river. He was seeing a splash in the water and the body of his brother Barney was sinking beneath the waves.

"The Sioux, the Cheyenne, and the Arapaho were all enemies once," Harper said. "They have now joined together and the Bluecoats cannot defeat them."

O'Leary was shaking his head. "I can see it all over again here. It will happen to these people as it did to us, don't you see. They can band together and be as strong as you please, but there'll come a day when they've got no food. The army will see to that, you can be sure. They'll kill all of these magnificent buffalo and then there'll be no fight. A man don't have no war left in him when his baby son is lyin' dead in his arms. I seen it many a time, me boy." He shuddered.

Overhead the twilight had given way to a nearly full moon whose brightness lit up the land with a soft white. The buffalo had bedded down and but for a few cows who bawled for lost calves, all was still but the soft breeze of nightfall.

O'Leary pulled a large penny whistle from his army coat and explained to Harper that he had just finished carving it from a piece of hollow wood he had found along the river. He played on it for a time, nodding with satisfaction that his efforts had been worthwhile.

"Get out your whistle," he said to Harper, "and teach me that love song."

Harper told him that he had destroyed the penny whistle. When O'Leary was silent, Harper explained that playing only reminded him of something he had lost and now wished only to forget. O'Leary worked into a bouncy Irish tune and stopped in the middle of it with a grunt.

"You know, me boy, it ain't been long past when ye told me I should learn to take me joy out of the land and not go around feelin' sorry for meself." He took another penny whistle from his pocket and handed it to Harper. "Now, I want to learn that pretty little song you was playin' the other night and I want to learn it now." He winked at Harper and added, "And don't let me catch ye breakin' any more o' the whistles I give ye. They don't grow on trees out here."

Harper smiled. "I will keep this one always. It is better than the last one you gave me. Now listen and I will teach you the song."

CHAPTER 4

The next day Harper read sign that the war party had returned. The change in the air could be felt by everyone and a state of uneasy tension dropped over them like a bank of fog. Harper ordered the wagons circled well before sundown and allowed no trips to the river for wood or water. When the sun finally went down, drums began to sound.

Many of them had heard drums before and old memories pushed their terrible way back into their minds. Looks of anger rushed into men's faces, as if they were seeing again what had likely happened the year before somewhere back along this long and regrettable trail. Their women, remembering also, stared through eyes that were crazy and helpless, while hands muffled cries from their lips. Some had dropped to their knees. Oglala drums mixed with those of the Cheyenne. There were many warriors and a great leader was among them. Their medicine would be good when the sun returned again.

Harper allowed water and wood to those who wished to get it. The drums were distant and there would be no warriors nearby; they were all preparing for what would come once the sun again rose over their vast hunting grounds, on the ragged edge of which stood the small wagon train. As Harper thought more about it, he realized their position was of no real relevance to the Sioux cause of protecting their northern territories. The strong notion that he was the reason for this sudden change seemed more and more probable: he, far more than any other of those who had been given back to the Bluecoats, knew their ways of war and their secret camping places. He knew how they thought

and what their secret medicines were. If he became angry and turned against them, it could prove very costly to them.

When the sun rose, the hills above the circle of wagons were lined with painted warriors. They were a mixture of Sioux and Cheyenne, led by a very prominent warrior of strength who was high in honor among the Oglala. His name was Red Cloud.

The sun was a ball of gold behind them as they sat on their horses and talked among themselves. They pointed down and shook their heads and argued. It was hard for them to fully understand what had happened below them, for Harper had ordered the men and women inside the wagons late the night before. Now there was only O'Leary and Harper, alone in the middle of the circled wagons, seated cross-legged together as if in council.

"That's a sunrise to behold," O'Leary said to Harper, looking into the sky over the warriors' heads. "A man don't realize what he sees and thinks nothin' of each day."

"This day will not be your last," Harper told him with confidence. "Already they wonder about their medicine. They do not know how many guns await them in each of the wagons. This will change their thinking and maybe they will decide not to fight."

"There's a good bunch of them," O'Leary said. He had his diary out. "How many should I put down? Six hundred?"

Harper smiled. Even in times of the greatest strain, O'Leary couldn't be serious.

"Why do you want to record so many?" Harper asked.

"I've never in me life seen so many Injuns. And the Good Lord knows if they all come down here at once I won't have time to count them all."

"I do not believe they will come down until they have first had council with us. It will give them more honor if they first tell me they will kill me."

O'Leary stared at him. He finally said, "You plan to go out there and let them tell you how you're goin' to die?"

"I do not plan to die. This I will tell them. I have many winters to see yet before I leave this life. Before I am finished in council with them, they will understand that many of their warriors will sing their death songs this day if they wish to end my life."

"You're hardly able to scare, are you me boy? But I can't see how you plan to put the fear to them, not with as many as they be."

"When a boy first goes into training to become a warrior, he is sent out alone to face the powers on his own. There are many things against him: heat, storm, wind, cold, loneliness. Many things that try both the mind and the body. To become a warrior the boy must overcome these things by telling himself he is strong enough to survive and to gain honor throughout his life. Once this inner power is gained, it is very difficult for the boy to ever lose his faith in himself. If he is from that day forward true to himself and to *Wakan' Tanka,* he can survive all tests of the mind and spirit. Among the Bad Face band of Oglala I was known to have gained much strength and honor as a very young boy and also a warrior. They already know that I have no fear of their numbers and when I tell them they are foolish to even be here, they will talk among themselves about fighting. The only one who concerns me is the one called Red Cloud. He has powerful medicine."

"I've heard talk of him at the fort."

"Already he is known as one of the greatest warriors among all the Sioux peoples," Harper said. "It is possible he will be a respected leader in time."

O'Leary was writing in his diary. Harper, still watching the warriors on the hill, let his eyes wander across the line of painted figures, naked except for breechclouts. Paint of red, yellow, and green was most common among them, together with some white and black, and occasionally blue. O'Leary remarked he had never seen anything like it and his eyes began to take on the stare of fear. He closed his diary and

put it into his pocket. Then he got to his feet and began to pace back and forth, clenching and unclenching his fists. He stared up at the warriors and talked under his breath.

"O'Leary, you have to face this," Harper told him. "You are the only real help I have."

"Don't depend on me."

"I have to. You must help me. Do anything you have to, but calm down. Go to the wagons and tell the men to keep their women quiet. Red Cloud will think they are all children and he will laugh while he fits an arrow to his bow." Harper added a final command. "Tell the men there is to be no shooting unless I order it. Those who disobey will be killed by me."

Harper took a Springfield musket and climbed upon one of the wagon seats, facing the line of warriors on the hill. He fired it into the air in the accepted signal that he wished to talk, that his rifle had already been fired and was not ready to use. There was no sign from the warriors that any of them wished to talk. Instead one warrior rode quickly from their ranks and pulled his horse to a stop in front of Red Cloud. Harper watched as the two talked and Red Cloud finally nodded his head.

The lone warrior descended the hill on his pony, chanting a personal medicine song. The horse was painted with red zig-zags to signify speed. Small half-circle yellow marks across the shoulders told Harper that this warrior had been on many horse raids. The warrior himself was painted red and yellow from head to foot. He carried a long coup stick striped with red and lined with scalps and the feathers from a black eagle. He was clearly a brave warrior with many honors, and he was Cheyenne.

Harper continued to stand on the seat of the wagon while the warrior made sign that he would gain honors this day by proving to all that the one called Sun Hair, who was once a warrior among the Bad Face band of Oglala Sioux, was but a child and not worthy of the honors he had once gained.

Harper repeated back in sign that it was strange a Cheyenne warrior would risk his own honor by challenging someone who was leaving the land. Maybe, Harper made sign to the warrior, he wanted to be laughed at, for it would be bad for him to challenge the one the Oglala once called Sun Hair.

With a loud whoop the warrior eased his pony into a gallop and circled the wagons at a distance. The emigrants all came out to watch and the warriors on the hill, including Red Cloud, chanted to urge him on. The pony broke from a gallop into an all-out run and the warrior eased in closer to the wagons with each circle his pony made. The intensity of his medicine song had increased with the speed of the horse and he began to slide from one side to the other and jump to the ground, springing back up over the rear of the horse, holding tightly to the mane as he performed. The wagon people were stunned and the warriors on the hill cheered.

The warrior continued, sliding underneath the belly and between the churning legs, twisting his coup stick through his fingers and switching it from hand to hand with incredible skill. Harper knew the act was soon to end with the most important part and if the warrior counted coup, he and all the wagon people would die this day.

The warrior suddenly swung his pony in close to the wagons and reached out with his coup stick to touch Harper. The striped stick passed under Harper's feet as he jumped quickly. The warrior drew his churning pony back around the circle of wagons for another pass. As he approached, the chants from the warriors on the hill grew increasingly louder. Again Harper jumped the stick. Now he gripped the Springfield rifle firmly by the barrel and waited for the next pass.

The warrior came in on his pony, brushing the wagons and yelling in his loudest voice. Harper waited. The coup stick was raised high. Harper ducked and swung the Springfield in an arc as the warrior passed, catching him flush in the face with the butt. The coup stick flew wildly into

the canvas cover of the wagon and bounced off. The warrior had flipped backwards off his pony and was rolling over and over slowly on the ground in front of the wagon, leaving marks of red where his face touched the trampled grass.

Harper took the pony's rawhide reins and led him to the warrior, down on his hands and knees, his head hanging while strings of vomit trailed from his mouth and nose. Harper left the Springfield against the wheel of the wagon and took a long look up on the hill before he helped the warrior onto his pony. There was no movement among the Indians on the hill so Harper took the reins and placed them in the warrior's trembling hands. His eyes were dull, the pupils widely dilated, and he made sign to Harper that Snow Fawn was his wife.

Harper stared after the warrior, clinging to his pony, till he reached the others on the hill. They began to care for him while Harper once again loaded the Springfield and fired it into the air. Red Cloud and two other warriors came part way down the hill. Harper borrowed a horse from a staring emigrant man and told O'Leary to see if he could make them relax. In a moment he had a penny whistle out and was dancing and playing. It was a strange sight, Harper thought: laughing children, stunned men and women, and angry warriors on the hill.

Harper greeted Red Cloud and the two stared without words for a time. They would not talk of the past, or even concede that they were from the same band. They would talk only of fighting.

"Who is that Bluecoat down among the wagons?" Red Cloud asked. "What manner of man plays and dances before he dies?"

"He is playing to the spirits," Harper answered. "They are with him this day, Red Cloud. The spirits are with all of us this day. You should be able to see that by now."

"You are afraid for those people who hide in the wagons,"

Red Cloud said. "You are afraid to see them die. And you are afraid to die. This proves that you are truely a *Wasicun*."

"It is strange," Harper told him in a strong tone of voice, "that you would risk warriors of your people to fight against wagon people who are almost out of the buffalo hunting grounds. This does not make sense when even as we speak Bluecoats travel to look for those warriors who attacked a train over against the mountains. Tell me, Red Cloud, are these *Wasicun,* who are afraid and leaving these lands, that important to you? Will your warriors gain many honors this day or will many of their women sing songs of mourning before another moon comes?"

Red Cloud was not one to be intimidated by anyone. His mind and body had passed many tests of skill and endurance and he was a man of strong convictions. It was plain to him that Harper's medicine was strong this day and the words about the lack of honor in killing trembling *Wasicun* were true, but a far greater glory awaited the warrior who won the scalp of the man who had once been Oglala himself, who had once been called Sun Hair.

"My skin is not the color of the Oglala people, but my war honors are many," Harper finally said to the silent Red Cloud. "If this is the day when I am to sing my death song, I will do so with honor. And many of these warriors with you will die by my hand. I feel sure that you do not want to fight this day yourself, but I can sense that you would be happy to see me fall at the hands of another. But you have seen that my medicine is strong, and will remain strong. To allow more warriors to become injured or die would be foolish."

"It was Elk-Dancing-at-Night who formed this war party," Red Cloud spoke up. "They followed you for the passing of three suns and came to get me. I was told that my medicine would break yours. This did not happen. But it is for each warrior to decide if he now wishes to go back or fight. Elk-Dancing-at-Night has lost his power. As for me, you have

spoken with wisdom in knowing I have not come to fight. To kill you would bring no additional honor to me, but only scowls from those who have said I was angry with Standing Bull for keeping you because I did not want you among the people. When you were given to the Bluecoats it was understood among us that you did not want to leave and were forced out. Unless you were to come back and fight against us, it would be dishonorable to kill you.

"But that is not the reason Elk-Dancing-at-Night brought us all together against you. He is not bound by our code among the Bad Faces. You know why he has come, Sun Hair. He says that he sees your face in the eyes of his wife, Snow Fawn. He says that your powers have their hold over her heart. He wanted those powers for himself and all these warriors came this day only to watch and to gather power for themselves when Elk-Dancing-at-Night counted coup against you. They would have all touched him and felt of the coup stick, so that some of the power could be theirs. Now they can only watch over him while he Walks in the Evening."

Harper now looked over to where Elk-Dancing had fallen unconscious upon the ground. His mind had indeed gone to Walk in the Evening, and there was no shaman among them who might say if he would come back or eventually die. They would take him back on a travois and it would be up to *Wakan' Tanka* to bring him back from his journey of the mind.

"I will go back to the *Wasicun,*" Harper announced to Red Cloud. "The fighting this day is finished."

Red Cloud and the other warriors watched as Harper descended the hill on his horse and went back in among the wagons. O'Leary had stopped playing the penny whistle and was smiling.

"Hold your head in pride, me boy. I don't know what you said to them but it must have been good. First time I ever saw a single man talk down six hundred. That'll be a whole page in me diary for sure."

There was yelling near one of the wagons and a rifle blast sounded. A warrior from among those on the hill dropped from his pony and all stared in stunned silence. Harper rushed over and grabbed the arm of a man named Dawson who was trying to reload the rifle. Harper pushed his back against a wagon and wrestled the rifle from him. With a short powerful stroke he then slammed the butt into the man's jaw and let him drop to the ground while he rushed out in front of the wagons and made sign to Red Cloud on the hill.

Harper told Red Cloud the man would be delivered to them and dragged Dawson out in front of the wagons a distance and dropped him. The warriors were all screaming for revenge and two were selected to go down and pick up the *Wasicun* lying on the ground. Harper went back into the circle of wagons and ordered all of them to the far side. He told those who yelled in anger at him that the warriors would now be satisfied and to be glad there would be no attack against the wagons. One so foolish as Dawson could have cost many lives.

Two warriors from the hill started their ponies down at a gallop. One of them had an old Hawken rifle from the fur trade days and the other had a Springfield musket he had no doubt taken from a dead soldier. They rode low over the backs of their horses, aiming their rifles at Dawson as he came to his knees and shook his head.

Screaming and yelling began again as a small girl ran out from the wagons toward Dawson, yelling, "Daddy! Daddy!" O'Leary gave a shout and pushed himself over a wagon tongue and out after the girl. Other men started forward and Harper screamed at them, explaining if any more went out the entire force would come down the hill and no one would survive.

Biting his lip, Harper loaded the Springfield he had taken and rushed out after O'Leary. Dawson had been shot in the head and the warriors were turning their ponies to O'Leary,

who had just scooped up the small girl. Before Harper could fire, the Hawken sounded. O'Leary spun sideways and fell, still clutching the kicking little girl. The other warrior, who's Springfield had already been fired into Dawson's face, used the butt to swing against O'Leary as he stumbled and tried to run. But he was falling and the little girl took the blow against the side of her head. Her legs stopped kicking and O'Leary fell across her.

Harper's Springfield spit flame and the warrior with the Hawken threw his arms skyward and let his head fall back as a round hole spewed blood along his spinal column. The other warrior turned his pony in a short circle and came back as Harper worked to reload the rifle. The warrior came and Harper threw the pouch of lead balls and the powder aside; he would have no time to finish reloading. The warrior had thrown his own empty rifle down and was fitting an arrow to a bow he had taken from across his back. Harper held the Springfield by its barrel and stood facing the oncoming horse, dodging from side to side as the warrior switched his bow from one side of the pony's neck to the other in an effort to aim and release an arrow. With the horse and warrior nearly upon him, Harper swung the rifle in a vicious arc and rolled sideways. The arrow zipped over his back and the pony jerked sideways. The warrior nearly fell, but caught himself as the horse danced in panic. Harper rushed up from behind and grabbed the warrior by his long hair, drawing a knife across his throat with a quick stroke. The warrior fell back and ran like a chicken across the ground before he fell and lay still.

Harper held the pony and looked up along the hills. The war party was not coming, but yelling and pointing toward the east. Two warriors came down and picked up the fallen, paying no attention to Harper as he stood with the pony. They wrapped their long war ropes through loops in the warriors' breechclouts and dragged the bodies up the hill to join the others. Red Cloud ordered them to hurry and took

one last cold look down at Harper before he turned his pony. In the distance a signal horn was sounding and a line of blue made its way toward the circled wagons.

Harper turned and saw O'Leary walking slowly toward him. Tears streamed from his eyes and the small girl lay against his chest, her arms hanging loosely, her head flopping awkwardly. There was a neat round hole in his blue uniform jacket just over the heart.

"How is it you are alive?" Harper asked.

"God in heaven knows. He wanted the little one. Not me."

Some of the emigrant men came up and took the small girl from O'Leary's trembling arms. They glared at Harper and one of them said that none of it would have happened if he had let well enough alone. He shouldn't have clubbed Dawson and given him to the savages. Harper told them about Indian law, but they turned and left.

O'Leary dried his eyes. "Wish I knew the reason for things as they happen. Don't seem quite fair at times."

Harper opened O'Leary's uniform and saw that the Hawken ball had demolished the large penny whistle he had just made. Splinters had pushed themselves into O'Leary's skin but the ball had glanced off. There was the beginning of swelling where a bruise was forming over his heart and the splinters had thin trails of blood reaching down from them. Harper began removing them while O'Leary stood in numbed silence.

"Your coat has great medicine," Harper told him as he pulled splinters. "It is a medicine coat."

"It's an old blue army uniform coat," O'Leary grunted. "God just put a penny whistle under it today." He shook his head. "I figure I'll have to make another one now and learn that song you taught me all over again."

Harper had finished removing the splinters and was feeling the coat, probing the hole the Hawken ball had made through the material.

"This coat has saved your life this day. Without it you

would not have had the whistle, for it was the coat that held the whistle. It is a good omen to have such a coat as this."

O'Leary shrugged. "I wish it would have helped out that small girl as well."

The emigrants had taken the bodies of Dawson and his small daughter into the circle of wagons. O'Leary explained to Harper that, as he understood it, Dawson had lost his wife and a son in a raid some time the summer before. He and the little girl had been wandering all over Oregon ever since and Dawson had finally decided to leave the West. His one last chance to get even had come and he wasn't going to pass it up. But it had cost him his life and had robbed his little daughter of a chance at life. Harper felt bad about the girl but knew Dawson was better off.

The soldiers were coming at a gallop across the last short distance to the wagons when Harper held the reins for O'Leary to take.

"You're about to find yourself in the army again if you don't get on this horse."

O'Leary shook his head. "You get on that horse, me boy. You need it worse that I do." He was looking at the emigrant men circle around the bodies of Dawson and the little girl. They were yelling and nodding and pointing at Harper. Some were loading rifles while others ran out to greet the soldiers, looking back over their shoulders as they went. "I figure they want your hide, lad. Get on the horse and be gone!"

"What about you? They don't treat deserters kindly."

"Ah, hell, I'll just say I was left to guide the train. Nobody knows different, you see." He stripped off his blue uniform jacket and shoved it into Harper's hands. "Have it, me boy. Big medicine!" He winked. "I'll miss you, you know."

Harper then gave O'Leary his own buckskin shirt. "Then take this so you will look like a scout. Good medicine to you. I will see you at another time, my friend."

Several of the soldiers had started toward them and the

emigrant men were coming from the wagons. O'Leary pretended he had been shoved to the ground and Harper headed north into the hills on the pony. There were shouts and shots and some of the cavalry gave chase for a short distance before it became evident they would never catch the Indian pony nor the white Indian hunched down over its back.

Harper eased the horse to a stop on a rise far out from the river. The wagons were now circled lumps of white in the distance while little blue specks milled around them. Once again Harper turned toward the west, but only for a last deep breath. He had killed Oglala warriors this day and was now their enemy; this had been said strongly in Red Cloud's eyes. He would have to leave this land and become what they had themselves forced upon him. He would now have to become a *Wasicun* and live in a world he knew nothing about. But there would come a day, he knew, when he again returned to this land. He would again see the sun fall over the mountains he had come to love and he would once more be a part of the earth and sky and four directions. He did not know when that day would come, but he did know his medicine would have to be good. He decided he would now insure that this medicine would be here waiting for him.

Harper circled back and came to a place down the trail from the wagons where a large sandstone rock stood prominently near the crossing point on the South Platte River. Here, in the twilight, Harper wrapped his blue medicine coat in a parfleche case he took from the pony and buried it where he knew he could find it. He said a prayer of thanks to *Wakan' Tanka* for his deliverance from the Bluecoats and the wagon people and climbed back on the pony, turning it east and wondering if O'Leary was busy carving another penny whistle.

Part Two

Our deeds still travel with us from afar,
And what we have been makes us what we are.

George Eliot

CHAPTER 5

He walks among those called bad by other Wasicun, *thieves and killers who have been put in this place as punishment. He has come from the alleys and the backroads; he has ridden the rails through many places and has found them all to be the same. They despise him for what he believes and for where he once lived. His blond hair is stringy and unkempt and the brightness in his blue eyes has been lost in the darkness of his cell. Most do not know his name and all leave him alone.*

Out from this prison a sudden and swift change is about to take place. The land and the people are torn in two by a conflict that divides the North from the South. There is little concern now about the lands to the west, for the soldiers have nearly all come back from the forts to fight an army dressed in grey. But the only battle Harper knows is the one within his mind that began when he heard, some five winters past, of a Bluecoat strike against a band of Cheyenne at a place called Sand Creek—the Little Dried River. The news was that all had been killed. In his mind he will always see Snow Fawn and Fox Boy walking beside him, both happy and relaxed, never again wanting to be apart. He fights this vision daily. The fighting now continues.

Now he spends his days remembering the past and the joys he once knew. He thinks also of O'Leary and wonders if he has found the life he was looking for. He plays O'Leary's penny whistle at times and it eases the isolation of solitary confinement. He must always be here for whenever he is let out into the courtyard, there is someone waiting to fight him who has heard he is Indian. Things here cannot change.

The leader of this prison has met with him before and has told him there can be no more fighting and hurting of other inmates. There is to be an agreement reached that will make everyone happy. It is hard to believe, for there have been many promises . . .

57

There was the click of a key in the lock and Harper found himself being escorted down the long row of cells and into the main prison yard. It was several minutes before his eyes could adjust to the light and by the time they had, he was taken down another corridor and asked to take a chair in front of the warden's desk. Harper turned his head to look outside, where birds sang in the early sunshine.

"Harper, I see your situation here as fairly serious," the warden began. "You have done it all, Harper. Beat up other prisoners, beat up guards. Tried to escape. Everything. Everything, that is, but kill somebody so that you will hang. No, you won't kill anybody. You just beat them up so bad they're never the same. Can you hear me, Harper?"

Harper turned from the window. "I hear you." He turned back again.

One of the guards who had brought him to the office was standing nearby thumping his heavy nightstick into the palm of his hand. "I think he needs a lesson in manners, warden."

The warden watched the guard for a few moments without expression. Then he told him, "You can go for now."

The thumping of the nightstick stopped and the guard looked puzzled.

"Go have some coffee," the warden nodded. "I'll call you if I need you."

The door to the office closed and the warden stood up from his desk and paced the floor.

"Harper, I haven't figured you out yet. On the outside you're a hard, stubborn man. But underneath it all I'm not so sure. If you could get the bitterness out of your system, I believe you could contribute a great deal to this society. Don't you want that?"

Harper spoke without turning from the window. "It doesn't matter what I want. I once lived with Indians. So I'm an Indian."

"But you're *not* an Indian."

"I've met a lot of people who would argue."

"You've just been around the wrong people, that's all."

"They all seem to be wrong for me."

"You're just not trying hard enough, Harper. That's all there is to it."

Harper turned from the window. "Get to the point, warden. What is it you want to say to me?"

The warden pointed to the door and shook his finger. "That man who was just here, that guard? Well, he's new here and he's a friend of some politician somewhere. He's bucking for my job and everybody knows it. He's known to be rough on prisoners, especially Indians."

"What does that matter? There are many like him."

"What I'm trying to say, Harper, is that if he comes after you there will be a whole lot of trouble in it for me. You'll break his arms and legs and his politician friend will think I put you up to it."

"Transfer me."

"Damn you, Harper, don't play with me! You know there's not a system in this country will take you. This is the last of them all. This is the worst."

"So what do you want?"

The warden placed his fingertips atop his desk and leaned across toward Harper. The excitement glowed in his eyes.

"I want you to consider an option to staying here. To staying in any prison."

"What option?"

"Now that the Rebellion has been put down, the army is headed back west to fight Indians. You would like to get back at those redskins, wouldn't you? You would like to make them pay for what they've done to you, I know you would."

Harper sat quietly in the chair while the warden waited round-eyed for an answer.

"You mean join the army?"

"Yes, of course."

"No."

The warden pushed off the desk and shrugged his shoul-

ders lightly. "Well, there's another option to this plan, Mr. Harper. I have a friend who runs a work camp for a plantation owner way down south, way down in the swamps. Harper, I mean this is deep in the swamps. He owes me a favor. He's always looking for good work stock and he doesn't care what color they are." He watched Harper with a grin working at his mouth. "The 'gators are as thick as flies down there and it's easy for a man to get lost. Those who don't work good get lost. I figure you'd rather go west than south, Harper. Am I right?"

Harper turned back toward the window and nodded his head.

The warden clapped his hands and uncovered some papers on his desk. He found a pen and shoved the whole mess around in front of Harper.

"I know you can sign your name now. In fact, I heard you was learning to write. Good, Harper. Write about your Indian friends. So if you'll just put your name on these lines I have marked, it will all be proper."

Harper was taken back to his cell and told there would be someone by to get him before long. There were others going as well, he learned. It was unusually noisy in the main part of the prison that night, for there were a lot of inmates going west to fight Indians. Harper took out his penny whistle and thought about O'Leary and the place called Courthouse Rock, where he had buried a blue medicine coat many winters past.

Harper was inducted into the second battalion of the Eighteenth U.S. Infantry in early May of 1866. He was now a member of the historical military force being sent into Indian lands to establish forts and protect emigrant wagon trains on their way to the gold fields of Montana. Colonel Henry B. Carrington, the commander of the newly established Mountain District, had assumed the duties of insuring safe passage to all *Wasicun* people who traveled the

Virginia City Road, which many were now calling the Bozeman Trail. This trail had been made since his leaving the Oglala, and he understood that it crossed squarely through the buffalo grasslands. Good hunting grounds were a reason to make war; already many of the *Wasicun* who had tried to cross had found it a good day to die.

He had been taken to Fort Kearney, Nebraska, where the regiment was billeted before beginning its march. His uniform had been salvaged from the North-South conflict, complete with two bullet holes in the blue wool sack coat and one in the kersey trousers. Dried blood stained the cloth around the holes. Harper did not favor wearing a dead man's uniform and was told he had no choice by the recruiting officer. It was the beginning of his steady battle against authority.

While the regiment settled into the task of preparing for the journey westward, Harper quarreled with the commanding officers. He would not settle into the routine of marching in basic military formation and refused to consider learning drills. He spent much of his time in the guardhouse with drunks and fighters who had found their way into uniform. When the officers learned he knew more about Indians than anyone else among them, they chose to allow him more leeway. There was a definite shortage of men who could scout and who knew the country and the Indian peoples themselves. He could be a vital source of information during the march into hostile territory. It was the way of the *Wasicun*: play a game of false reverence to someone from whom you might wish to gain.

Harper began to make evening journeys to nearby hills above the fort where he could see the endless stretch of land toward the west. It had been a long time since he had been able to look so far into the distance and it frustrated him to realize that his eyesight had regressed. It would come back to him, he resolved, for never again would he allow himself to be held within the confines of any boundaries whatsoever.

He played the penny whistle more each day while his mind tried to sort out the complex ties of his once again changing life. He wondered at the strange twists of fate that had torn him from the Oglala and delivered him to the land of the *Wasicun* and was now sending him back as a Bluecoat soldier, as if he were a doll being passed from hand-to-hand to be treated in a strange manner by each who took him. There were times when he wished he had not agreed to leave the prison and had taken his chances in the swamps to the south. He wondered if death would have found him there, in a land he had never seen and knew nothing of. He knew in reality that he would have lived and would have escaped, only to live knowing that someone was always looking for him. Here no one cared what he did and perhaps it was better.

No matter how he chose to think about it, Harper felt strange inside. He was going back to a land where he had once been happy, but now contained only memories of those he wished to forget. Snow Fawn and Fox Boy broke through his sleep each night. He wished he could think of Fox Boy as a young man ready to make his first vision quest, skilled with bow and arrow and an expert horseman. He wished his dreams would bring the boy to him with eagle feathers in his hair and a singer standing behind him, telling the village of this young man's glory among them. Instead his thoughts and dreams were scarred with the look in Snow Fawn's eyes that night outside Fort Laramie when she held a small boy in her arms and told him how it was to give birth to a son with no father to hold him up to *Wakan' Tanka*.

Things could never change now; it had ended at Sand Creek. He thought now that he was one of them, the same as Chivington and the men who had killed them, a Bluecoat soldier. It made him sick and it made him want to scream. But then he thought of the day he had been forced out and was happy he was going to return and take vengeance on those who sent him away. His adopted father, Standing Bull, and the others in the Bad Face band of Oglala people, who

had all watched with indifference that day when he had been ransomed for horses, would all see him once again. It will be a great surprise to them, and they will sing their death song, each one. Perhaps fate had put him in the right place after all. As a Bluecoat he would again ride to the village and again see their eyes, which would now be filled with fear. He would fight them all, and they would be sorry they had been foolish enough to send him away.

What many were now calling "Carrington's Overland Circus" pulled out of Fort Kearney, Nebraska, on the morning of May 19th. Harper had been placed among the ranks and not in front to scout as he had initially been told. They had acquired the services of another in that position and once again Harper's life crossed with that of Jim Bridger. Bridger had been guiding Deals the day Harper had been taken from the Oglalas and it all came back to him again, as well as his last days with his parents on that desert when Bridger had been gone and the wagons had found the poisoned water. It seemed odd to Harper how one man could be so innocently related with the worst times of another man's life.

The train of soldiers and settlers and wagons slowly began to string itself out along the wheel-etched south bank of the Platte River. Six-mule teams pulled two hundred and twenty of the white-cloth wagons and a number of the Bluecoat ambulance wagons. Besides the food and loads of firearms, ammunition, and other military supplies, there were washing machines, chairs, butter churns, expensive china and silverware, beds, glass windows, and many other personal possessions belonging to wives, cooks, and servants. There were chickens and hogs and a church bell brought for Sunday services, and cattle and horses in great numbers. All this was led by Carrington and his officer escorts, his wife and the wives of other officers and men, together with Carrington's personal marching band, which scattered the livestock for a few days until they became accustomed to the noise.

Harper watched it all and began to find himself very much amused. Everything seemed funny about these Bluecoats and wagon people who soon became lost in this land of endless open grass and boundless skies. Most complained about the lack of trees and water in this dry part of the world where rain fell far less than it did in the lands they were used to. Some of the women, including Carrington's wife, kept diaries of the journey, recording their impressions of the turbulent river and their anxieties regarding where life was taking them. Indians had been their main concern before the beginning of the march, and now it was the noise and dust and squalid air of hot animals and men.

They reached the South Platte River and the post that had been built there called Fort Sedgwick. Three days were spent towing the wagons across the river through a channel filled with quicksand. Once again Harper thought of O'Leary and the wagon people who had wanted to kill him for the deaths of Dawson and his little girl, now seven winters past. O'Leary had certainly saved him that day from the rifles of the emigrants. Even if someone among the Bluecoats had prevented it, they would have found a way to hang him later. He had left on a pony meant for O'Leary's escape and now he could only wonder if the Irish soldier with the thin red hair and the dancing smile had ever made it out of the army.

While the camp was silent the third night, Harper made his way out to where he had buried the medicine coat O'Leary had given him. He found it easy to sneak past the sentries and quietly worked his way to the base of the large sandstone rock he had used as a landmark.

The digging was easy in the soft sand at the base of the rock and he found the parfleche bag damp on the outside, but dry and clean within where the coat had been placed. He stripped his uniform issue off and put his arms through the coat O'Leary had given him. It was cool for a time but felt very good. As he got ready to return he stopped and hid

himself. Whoever was there was very quiet; as quiet as an Indian.

"Harper, I would like to talk. No harm intended to you."

The voice was Bridger's. He walked closer with his hand raised in the dim light of the half moon overhead, the sign for peace. He could not figure where Harper was hidden and spoke again.

"I aim only to talk, if you'll have it that way." He pulled his knife and dropped it from over his head.

Harper stood up. "How do you know my name?"

"I remembered the face and I found out the name. I want to say right off that when I led Deals to your village I had no idea that the Bad Faces would really give up their captives. Especially you. I don't want you mad at me and lookin' for a way to put a knife across my throat."

"If I wanted revenge it would be against Deals, not you."

"If you want it, you'll get the chance before long. I hear he went out to Laramie with Connor last year and that he's jumped rank clean up to colonel. But if I was you, I would figure just to stay clear of him. He's out on special assignment and he wants to make a name for himself. Those kind are big trouble."

"I can understand why you would want to be sure I did not want to kill you," Harper said, "but why do you tell me all this about Deals?"

"Just tradin' for a favor," Bridger said. "Or hopin' to."

"A favor?"

"I need you up front for me, to help with Carrington. I can't make him hear a word I tell him and I've got no time to do all the scoutin' and talkin' that needs to be done after today. If things ain't planned out right, there'll be a lot of trouble waitin' for us once we reach Laramie."

Harper fully understood what Bridger's worry was. Earlier in the day, while they had struggled to get the wagons across the river, they had been passed by another expedition

on its way to Fort Laramie. Harper had learned it was called the Peace Commission, and its intent was to meet with the leaders of the Plains Tribes and convince them to allow passage along the Powder River to emigrants traveling the Bozeman Trail. The tribes had agreed to assemble at Fort Laramie for council, where they would receive presents and food for their people. There would be talk about a solution to the fighting that was now taking place. It seemed odd to Harper that a group preaching peace was so closely followed by a force making war.

"Do you want to keep Carrington away from Laramie?" Harper asked.

Bridger shook his head. "I can't stop him or turn him back no matter what. I just want to slow him down. I want you to help by sayin' we've got to stop and meet with a war party that's on our tail."

"What makes you think he will listen to me if he pays no attention to you?"

"We've got to try. There's bound to be more Indians at Fort Laramie by the time we get there than a man's eye can take in. If they decide to make war, this army will be gone in less than a day. You know that."

Harper nodded. "I am not afraid to die."

"Well, it ain't my time yet," Bridger growled, "and I'd be obliged if you would think of other than your own hair for just a spell yet. At least until the council at Laramie is over."

"Maybe it would be best if the battle was fought right away," Harper suggested. "Then it would be settled, one way or another."

"That will not settle it," Bridger said with conviction. "If Carrington and all of us get wiped out, another force will be sent out within a week. There's no end to this thing. You've got to know that."

Harper took a deep breath. "Maybe you are right. Maybe there is no reason for everyone to die just so the Great Fathers in Washington can become angry and tell everyone

that they are right in saying the Indian peoples are animals. But I believe we are only putting off what will happen sooner or later."

"Let's wait till later," Bridger suggested. "Now, if you help me with this I won't tell Carrington I caught you out here."

"And if you won't tell Carrington I was out here, I won't cut your throat."

They both laughed and returned to the camp, going back to their beds with a quiet learned only from many years of fighting. No one had missed them and no one would know of their talk. Only they would understand that what the two of them decided in the days ahead would keep them from all being killed once they reached Fort Laramie.

Harper was brought up front to help Bridger and assumed his duties by taking a spotting glass and working out ahead of the column. The idea of slowing the column never developed, since Carrington was motivated to reach Fort Laramie and then travel up the Bozeman Trail as quickly as possible. His orders were to rebuild Fort Connor, now Fort Reno, and establish two new posts before the end of the summer. So the marching was brisk and there was not to be a slowdown unless an attack was made.

This made Bridger more nervous than ever and he spent his time watching the hills and telling Harper that he liked Carrington as a person but thought he knew squat about Indians. The men in ranks seemed to rise to the spirit of the schedule and looked forward to their duties as guardians of the westward movement. Past Courthouse Rock, Chimney Rock, and Scott's Bluff they marched, stepping in time to a cheerful set of lyrics mustered from an Irish tune:

> *The girls all cried and said goodbye,*
> *A likely lot are we.*
> *We stand in line and march in time*
> *To the gates of Laramie.*

> *On we go to the Bozeman Road*
> *All soldier lads are we.*
> *We'll save the day as we fight our way*
> *To the gates of Laramie.*

But the marching songs quieted when Bridger and Harper showed Carrington what they had been talking about the entire way. They were now four miles from Fort Laramie, looking out across the valley at an enormous gathering of Indians, so many that the eye could not see the end of them. Harper saw that five of the seven disparate divisions of the Teton Sioux were present: the Oglala, Minniconjou, Brulé, Hunkpapa, and Two Kettles, together with the Cheyenne and Arapaho peoples. The valley was filled with lodges; men, women, and children of all sizes moved about to discuss things and visit with relatives among the other bands and divisions. Dogs ran and barked, and a sea of brown and black and white ponies was strung across the slopes and through the bottom.

Harper listened as Carrington told Bridger his specific orders were to secure needed supplies at the fort and proceed on up to Powder River and beyond. He did not realize that the presence of so many women and children could drive the warriors to extremes should trouble break out. And he seemed not to understand that an Indian warrior could shoot four to five arrows at leisure in the time it took to reload the Springfield muzzle-loaders the troops were armed with. It was learned also that some of the warriors had the new breech-loading rifles they had acquired in trade or had taken from those on emigrant trains. They seemed to be better equipped for fighting than the army.

As the camp was made, the wagons drawn into a crude circle and the tents pitched, it became clear to Harper that he had joined an army that thought its presence was enough to intimidate any Indian, and it seemed odd that this army's leaders could not see how brightly dressed the Indian lead-

ers were themselves: feathers and paint and medicine ornaments symbolized the same thing as shoulder stripes and stars and polished brass buttons. It all meant honor and fearlessness. It meant there would be no backing down until many had seen their deaths.

CHAPTER 6

"You are Sun Hair, who was once in the Bad Face band of Oglalas. Why are you now a Bluecoat?"

The words were those of Spotted Tail, one of the Brulé leaders who had brought their people to the peace council. He was half-brother to Standing Bull, Harper's adopted father, and was surprised to learn that a Bluecoat army had been sent out right behind those *Wasicun* who had come calling themselves a Peace Commission.

"You wear the coat of an enemy," Spotted Tail added. "You will hear now from me that Standing Bull was killed before the last winter passed, fighting the white chief named Connor up on Powder River. Now you come, his adopted son, to fight your own people."

"It was they who threw me out," Harper said with irritation. "They sent me away when I had done nothing wrong. They traded me for horses in a foolish hope that the wagon people would then stay out of the buffalo grounds. So do not tell me who should be sorry."

"Then you intend to fight with the other Bluecoats?"

"I would be wearing the medicine of the red-tailed hawk even as we speak if I had not been sent away. Yes, I will fight."

Spotted Tail shrugged. "You will have to fight well, Sun Hair. Even better than you did as a Bad Face warrior. Many of those you learned war games with as a boy are now strong leaders: Crazy Horse, High Back Bone, and Yellow Eagle are all strong among the Oglala, with Crazy Horse gaining more honor each day. The Cheyennes, Black Horse, Two Moon, Dull Knife, and Little Wolf, they are all angry. Black Bear of

71

the Arapaho watched his people die at the hands of Star Chief Connor before the last winter. The people are all angry, and they are glad to see the young men gain strength and courage.

"And there are the older leaders who have listened to *Wasicun* lies for too long. Man-Afraid-of-His-Horses wants to fight. And there is Red Cloud. I do not have to speak of him to you, Sun Hair. Though he is growing older he is now ready for war. He has tried hard for peace, but his heart is now very angry. They have all come together and have forgotten any past problems between them. They have come together to fight, Sun Hair. You can tell that to the new white chief who has led you here."

"You must tell him yourself," Harper said. "And you will have to tell him where your people stand."

"War is not a part of my life. I am a peace chief, Sun Hair. You know that."

"Bluecoats do not know the difference," Harper said. "To them you are all the same."

Spotted Tail grunted. "I do not wish to talk with any of them. Standing Elk wants to be heard. Let him talk with the Bluecoat chief. I have said enough."

Spotted Tail pulled his blanket up close around him in a gesture of anger and walked away. He made his way back to the Brulé camp and Harper watched him confer with other leaders, throwing his hands and arms around and turning his head in short quick movements. Warriors from the many bands had been readying themselves for the conference and there were many shows of finely crafted war shirts and bonnets. All were painted from head to foot in their medicine colors. Besides the leaders mentioned by Spotted Tail, Harper recognized many others, the years seeming to have brought a hardness to their features that had not come with age. There was Sitting Bull, who was rising fast among the Hunkpapas; Hump and Thunder Hawk had acquired honor with the Minniconjous. They were all young and fearless,

and their feet itched to glide onto a pony and kick forward into battle.

Harper saw Bridger trying desperately to make Carrington understand that to interrupt the work of the Peace Commission would cause trouble and possibly fighting. Harper went over to assist Bridger and told Carrington that he should listen to what one of the Brulé leaders had to say. The warrior Standing Elk was dressing for council and would be over shortly to meet them at the officers' tent. Carrington finally consented to talk with Standing Elk, but made it clear that he intended to march his men the remaining distance up to Fort Laramie as soon as the detachment he had sent for ammunition arrived. Whatever Standing Elk might have to say was not important to Carrington; he had his orders and he was going to Powder River as soon as he was supplied from the fort.

Harper went off by himself and stood for a time, watching the reaction of the young warriors to the news and the evidence before their eyes that a new Bluecoat fighting force had come into these lands. It was certain that in time many of these younger Brulé warriors would leave their bands to join those who would fight. Standing Elk wanted to warn Carrington, Harper knew, because though his people had been friendly up to now, fighting would disrupt things even among the friendly bands. The Bluecoats would not know the difference and would cut off food and clothing allotments to all Sioux people. It seemed plain that Standing Elk would try and dissuade Carrington from going north along the Bozeman Trail, which would bring about certain war.

As Harper watched Standing Elk being dressed and decorated for council, he was joined by one of Carrington's commanding officers. The officer approached Harper briskly and cleared his throat.

"I would like a word with you, if I might. Though we have not spoken before, I am sure you know that I am William J. Fetterman and that I hold the rank of captain. To get to the

point, private Harper, I believe we can be of mutual benefit to one another. And do you intend to salute me, private Harper?"

"Carrington doesn't make me salute him."

"You mean *Colonel* Carrington."

"You know who I mean."

"Well, private Harper, I am not as lenient as the colonel and I—"

"Do you want to talk to me or put me under arrest?"

"Very well, private. I had heard you lacked respect, but aside from that I think we can help one another out a bit."

Harper listened knowing that whatever this particular commander had to say wasn't likely to be too practical in nature. Captain Fetterman's reputation as an Indian hater had already become widely known; but like Carrington, his knowledge of Indian warfare was next to nothing. It was said that he could not understand why Indians didn't charge like real soldiers do, and it was also said he felt he could ride through the entire Sioux nation with eighty good men. Harper had heard Carrington tell him more than once that there would be no detachments from the marching ranks to seek out hostile savages and destroy them. Perhaps Fetterman had won himself honor in the North-South conflict, during which soldiers charged ahead to certain death many times, but these were the buffalo grasslands where the Sioux people had hunted for many winters and where they would fight their own way.

"It is my understanding," Fetterman continued, "that you were captured as a small child and abused by these savages out here, and that you were subsequently rescued by Colonel Roland Deals, who is presently serving unattached at Fort Laramie. I am overjoyed to learn you want to extract revenge against them. And that, you see, is where we can be of service to one another."

"How do you know Deals?" Harper asked.

"I met him during the fighting at Shiloh. He is certainly

not the leader *he* thinks he is, though he has a lot of friends in the right places who let him get away with whatever he wants. From that standpoint, I envy him."

"And you're stuck under Carrington."

"I'm afraid so for now. I understand that I might change assignment here shortly, but it is not certain. In any event, I do not intend to let anyone or anything deter me from my military duties as a commander against hostile Indian forces. And, as I say, I was happy to learn you want to kill them off as soon as possible."

"Tell me, Captain Fetterman," Harper said matter-of-factly, "how do you intend to help me?"

Fetterman chuckled as if he appreciated a good joke. "You know this country, private Harper, and you know where the hostiles camp during the year. My thought is to go out and destroy their villages so they will have to spend all their time rebuilding and then will have no time left for war."

"Carrington is getting ready to tell Standing Elk in a few minutes that he did not come to make war, but only to guard the Bozeman Trail for the wagon people."

Fetterman cleared his throat. "But you and I both know we have to eliminate these people entirely to make this country suitable for civilization. Carrington is too soft. He is a good planner, but he is not a leader in any sense of the word."

"Why are you telling me all this?"

"I want your support when the time comes."

"Why not Bridger?"

"I want *you,* private Harper." Fetterman sounded like he was pleading. It was if his whole life were coming to a high point now and he did not want to fail in his quest. "I understand that you were a powerful young fighter among them at one time and that they fear you. And I know that Carrington has confidence in you. My plan will work, I know it will! If I were to take you and the cavalry north, while Bridger led Carrington and the rest of the infantry to the proposed fort locations, then we could eliminate the savages

and their homes while the forts were under construction. Don't you see? The savages would have to draw back from the Bozeman Trail to defend their homes and the construction process could then proceed at double-time. I am sure we would both be decorated highly!"

"Do you know how many warriors will be in those hills?" Harper asked.

"Does it matter? One good soldier is worth at least a dozen savages, and they certainly can't outnumber us beyond that. We'll also have a field cannon. We'll cut them down like a sickle through grass!"

Fetterman waved his arm in a wild circle and Harper motioned over toward Carrington and the other officers, who were now receiving Standing Elk of the friendly Brulés for the council. As they walked over, Fetterman said to Harper, "I want you to be ready to side with me when the time comes."

Harper sat with Bridger to interpret and the council with Standing Elk and his warriors began. The pipe was lit and passed around. Carrington puffed reluctantly, then Standing Elk began to speak.

"He wants to know where you are going?" Harper told Carrington.

Carrington's reply through Harper was that he was taking forces to the Powder River country to guard the road to Montana for the wagon people.

Standing Elk had prepared a warning, and Harper told it to Carrington. "There is a treaty being made with the Sioux that are in the country where you are going. They will not sell their hunting grounds to the white men for a road. You will have to fight the Sioux warriors if you go there, and they will not give you the road unless you whip them."

Carrington had Harper tell Standing Elk that his intentions were not to make war, but only keep the wagon people safe.

"The Brulé people are friends with their white brothers," Standing Elk then said through Harper. "But that is not the

way it is with Red Cloud's people, the Oglala, and the other peoples of the Sioux. Red Cloud did not want to come here to speak of peace, but came when he was told his people would receive presents and clothing for their backs. He will be very angry if you go into the fort where the council is being held. He will think you have come to fight. And he will be right."

There was nothing left to discuss on either side so Standing Elk paid his respects then led his warriors back to their camp. The Bluecoats began to relax since there would likely be no fighting here, even if Red Cloud and the other leaders became angered. The Brulés didn't want to get caught in the middle, and it had been learned that many of the younger fighting warriors had remained north along the Powder River. It was also evident that the hunting had been bad again this year and that most of the Indians were still trying to recover from the harsh winter and the lack of game. It was easy to see now that Red Cloud had been tricked into thinking his people would be cared for if he would agree to a lasting peace.

As darkness approached, Harper could hear Carrington conferring with his officers about attending the peace conference the following morning. Under the circumstances now evident to Carrington, there must be a display of strength shown to Red Cloud and the other leaders so that they understood he meant to carry out his orders and guard the Bozeman Trail. His plan was to march into the fort and be introduced to the Indian leaders. There was no question in Harper's mind now that this Bluecoat army was one filled with strange thinking and that this twisted line of reasoning was going to start the drums of war to sounding just as soon as Red Cloud and the other leaders of the fighting bands could return north to their villages.

Fetterman approached Harper again the morning after Carrington and the officers, together with the marching band and the scouts, had been invited to the peace council.

Fetterman began talking about his proposal to destroy villages and camps but was soon interrupted by the appearance of a man dressed in dark buckskins, wearing an English safari hat. Fetterman saluted him stiffly and then Colonel Roland Deals frowned at Harper.

"So we meet again, *private* Harper. I am so glad to learn you are here among us in uniform this time. I didn't see you salute."

"I didn't."

"That's insubordination, private."

"You will overlook it today, won't you, Deals? There is a peace conference going on and you don't want to disturb that, do you?"

Deals chuckled through his teeth and glared. "Of course, private. Only joking, I'm sure. Oh, and you will be glad to know that I acquired another paper with the story of your 'rescue' by myself and my forces. Please don't ask to see it."

"I believe we are due inside," Fetterman said.

Deals raised his eyebrows. "Indeed. I see no one else in any alarm." He turned his attention back to Harper. "You will be happy to learn I am planning an expedition similar to the one on which I first met you. I will be needing a scout and you will be perfect."

"He is assigned to Colonel Carrington's command, sir," Fetterman spoke up again. "I am quite certain it would be impossible to detach him."

Deals curled his lips. "Captain Fetterman, when I am interested in your opinions, I will ask for them. Is that quite understood?"

Fetterman gritted his teeth and saluted. "Yes, sir. Sorry, sir."

Deals turned back again to Harper. He knew better than to ask Harper if he wanted to go; there was no telling what kind of answer Harper might have and there was no point in being further embarrassed by this savage dressed in blue.

"It will be some time yet before all the arrangements can

be made," he said, squinting at Harper, "but when they are, I can assure you I will make whatever effort it takes to locate the post you've been assigned to. I don't care if I have to go all the way up to Virginia City, private Harper, you are going to be under my command just as soon as possible." He then grinned wickedly as he prepared to leave and join other commanders. "I believe I could even arrange to have more pictures taken. That would certainly be nice, wouldn't it?"

After Deals left, Fetterman asked Harper what he had done to incur such wrath from Deals.

"He is arrogant and self-serving," Harper answered. "And those kind of men are just asking to die."

Fetterman then left to join Carrington and his staff. It was plain that he was disturbed by the sudden interruption of his own plans by Deals and would likely try to get his mission underway as soon as possible. Not wanting to be a part of what was to come, Harper broke ranks and found a hill. He watched through his spy glass as Carrington and his officers strolled onto the parade ground where the peace conference was in session. Carrington saluted the fort commanders and extended his hand to a man in civilian clothes named Taylor, the head of the Peace Commission. Bridger stood back, his arms crossed, shaking his head, while the Indian leaders rose and began a display of anger.

Through the shouting and yelling, Carrington tried to tell them what he wanted them to hear, but the noise was too great. The Minniconjous and the Oglalas were defiant and realized immediately that the Bluecoats took them for fools. Harper trained his spyglass on Red Cloud while he stood and waved his arms, his face stone hard with anger as he spoke. Carrington came forward to meet him but Red Cloud turned his back and wrapped his blanket over his head and walked away. Others followed suit and the parade ground was soon empty of all but the Brulés, the Cheyennes, and the Arapahoes, many of whom were also talking of leaving. Carrington and the other commanders had been warned not

to bring their Bluecoat soldiers to the Powder River country. A war in earnest was about to begin.

The Bozeman Trail was a set of wagon ruts that twisted through draws and up steep hills, across creeks and streambeds white with salt, and seemed to go on forever through a land of wind and sagebrush and gumbo soil. The women wrote in their diaries about the hardships of life in a wagon train and their fear of the Sioux, who were preparing for war against all whites who came into this valley on their way to the gold fields of the Montana Territory.

Again they had to cross an unpredictable river, this time the North Platte, where a ferry took the wagons across while the herds swam. They moved on to where the road forked, the Mormon Road twisting off west toward Salt Lake City. Here Harper met French Pete, a trader who had a crude log shed, and asked him if he could remember the days when the Bad Face band of Oglala came with a white boy who spoke English. French Pete laughed for a moment and then gathered his half-breed children beside him and said he remembered, but that those days were past. He said the Oglala had come through not long before and that their eyes were filled with hate and they had asked if any wagons had come through. French Pete said no, and later asked that no one speak English around his trading post any more.

The wagons and the cattle and the soldiers pushed north-ward to establish forts and Harper watched the hills for warriors who could come at any time. They were at Powder River, he had learned from French Pete, holding the Sun Dance ceremony, and would be ready for war when it was finished. They wanted no more of the *Wasicun,* for they brought sickness and also the burning water that scrambled men's thoughts and made them reckless. The white man's whiskey was even more deadly than the rifle and the leaders had forbid its use among them. Still it found its way into the

villages and destroyed lives. They knew if they were to win this war against the Bluecoats they could not be reckless.

Once past the Laramie hills, the Bighorn Mountains finally came in sight and the last ridge was crossed before they reached their first stop. For nearly a week, all the soldiers had talked about was Fort Reno, the post that had been called Connor the year before. Now it lay before them on a high bench overlooking the Powder River, nothing more than a bracing of uneven logs discolored by dust and wind. Someone commented that Connor must have been suffering from the heat to pick this spot to build a fort. Another said it would take heat and something else along with it to be so crazy.

Carrington struck up the band and the column marched down the hill to wild cheers as soldiers from the post below streamed through the gates and emigrants from three waiting trains danced around their wagons. It seemed more like a family reunion than a mission to relieve and re-enforce an isolated military outpost. The soldiers there, as Harper learned, had remained over the winter against their will, a number having deserted notwithstanding the hostile Indians. Those in Carrington's force were calling them "white-washed Rebs," or more often, "galvanized Yankees." During the North-South conflict they had been Confederate prisoners of war who had come west to fight Indians rather than remain in Yankee prison camps. The end of the war had not meant the end of their enlistments and Fort Reno had become another detention camp for them.

Among them was a soldier whose red-grey hair had grown more grey with the years, but whose eyes still held the sparkle of fresh rain in the morning. He played tunes on his penny whistle for two young emigrants who had been married at sundown the day before. Harper watched him for a time and finally stopped his playing.

"Don't you know a white Indian when you see one?"

His mouth dropped and his eyes got huge and round and he jumped up to embrace Harper. Despite all the years, Mickey O'Leary's grin had widened.

"Well glory be and I'll be damned! This world ain't so big after all." He looked Harper up and down. "Have you growed, or I shrunk?"

"We've both shrunk," Harper said. "Only you more than me."

O'Leary was laughing and shaking his head. "I never figured to ever see you again, lad. But it's got to be you. No white Sioux ever looked ornerier. You fight in the war?"

Harper shook his head. "I sat through it in prison."

"You got thrown behind bars?"

"I just couldn't do things right for anybody, and I wouldn't let them step on me."

O'Leary slapped him on the shoulder. "Don't matter none now, me boy. Don't matter atall. You made your way out and you ain't dead yet. But keep ye fingers crossed, lad, the food and water here will do you under for sure."

"You must have fought as a Rebel."

"I took to workin' a travelin' show after I got away from that wagon train. Done pretty well, singin' and playin' the towns and such. Room and board and drinkin' money. The war broke out and a bunch of Bluebellies shot us up. I spent better'n a month lyin' on my back." He showed Harper a scar in his left side. "I still get trouble breathin' now and again. Just as soon as I was mended I got myself a grey uniform and a horse and took to warrin' against the Union. I figured anyone with no more sense than to shoot down an old Irish whistle player has got no call runnin' a country."

Harper laughed. "You should have had your whistle in your pocket to stop the bullet."

"Ah! I'll never ruin another whistle that way again, lad. Takes too long to make a new one."

"You fought with the Greycoats," Harper said with a shake

of his head, "and still you couldn't stay out of a blue uniform."

"Nothin' to laugh at, me boy. I found meself eatin' rat meat at a Yankee prison camp. They told me it was either more rat meat or put on the blue and come out here again to fight Injuns." He looked around and motioned to the scattered and poorly constructed quarters and storage sheds. "I'd have stayed a good sight warmer this past winter in the Yankee camp. And maybe rat meat ain't what a man considers a good meal, but it chewed better than the beans they put in front of us here."

"I would say your medicine was better than mine," Harper told him. "You recognize this coat?"

O'Leary watched Harper point to a bullet hole over the heart and chuckled. "How'd you manage to keep it all this time?"

"I buried it back at the South Platte Crossing, just after I outran the cavalry on that pony. I dug it up again when we marched through there. Things have gone better ever since I put it on again."

"Best you button it up right away," O'Leary said, pointing toward the horses. "It seems the guards at the herds came in to join the celebration and left the door open for the Injuns."

There were a number of yells from men scattered about and screaming women were taken within the shelter of the post. A war party of Oglala had swept down suddenly while everyone was busy celebrating and was running off mules and horses. Carrington ordered pursuit by nearly half the cavalry with Fetterman in command.

O'Leary was shaking his head. "They'll never catch them. They're headed toward Pumpkin Buttes, and that's to hell and gone. If they've got a lick of sense, they'll turn around before they get to the hills. Men don't come back from out there."

The cavalry returned the following morning with nothing

but an Indian pony loaded with cloth and beads from the
Fort Laramie Peace Commission. One of the men remarked
he had seen hell after the cinders had cooled. The Indians
had vanished late the night before and the soldiers had sat
up all night until it was light enough to travel back. They had
been lucky there was no war dance before the raid on the
livestock or they would have gotten their first taste of Oglala
warfare.

During the following week there was discussion about Fort
Reno. Carrington's orders were to rebuild it farther north,
but he was behind schedule as it was and finally decided to
leave a quarter of his force behind to rebuild what was
already there. Two more forts would have to be built farther
up before the end of summer and Bridger was finally getting
Carrington to understand that under the best of circumstances travel in this huge country was slow and awkward.

Harper again said goodbye to O'Leary as the column got
ready to leave. O'Leary had tried in vain to get reassigned to
Carrington's force and Harper tried to cheer him.

"They say there's a wagonload of paint coming up here
from Fort Laramie one of these days. Once this fort is
trimmed up some, maybe it won't be so bad."

O'Leary grunted. "Put a ribbon on a pig and what have
you got?"

Harper watched the soldiers and emigrant men argue and
saw the herders fighting to get the stock rounded up and
ready to drive in line with the column of wagons.

"Maybe you are lucky not to be going," Harper commented. "They don't call this whole thing a circus for nothing."

"Circus or not, I got me reasons for wantin' to go along,"
O'Leary whispered. "I figure this army will see no more of
Mickey O'Leary once I can get north a good piece. You see,
me boy, the fever of gold has got all these folks in these
wagons frothin' at the mouth, and a wee bit o' that sickness
has gotten into me."

Harper laughed and shook his head. "So I can plan to see you come out of a wagon again some day and tell me that you've left the army behind?"

"If I can find me the right wagon," O'Leary winked. "Take care of yourself, me boy, and wait fer me up the road."

CHAPTER 7

The Bighorn Mountains swelled high and rugged to the west, seemingly at arm's reach from the wagon trail that wound through the foothills along their base. Cloud Peak rose from mid-range to touch the blue ceiling of sky. Carrington was now searching for a place to have a fort constructed, to be named Fort Philip Kearny in honor of a Union officer slain in the battle of Chantilly in 1862. They were a week north of Fort Reno, in the heart of the northern hunting grounds, and the Sioux had found them. Each day as the wagons and the soldiers and the cattle moved past ancient sites of worship and sacred burial grounds, Harper watched the hills and the hundreds of warriors who came to see the Bluecoat soldiers march in defiance of their wishes. They made their medicine signs and discussed fighting, but this command was far too large to attack without great loss of life. They would wait and make many plans and have the Special Ones, those who were man-woman among them, do their dances and tell them when the fighting should begin.

Already in the seven winters since Harper had been among them, many young men had risen to warrior status. The main young warrior among them was Crazy Horse and he looked down at Harper daily with an air of interest. They had been friends and rivals as boys, and had grown up learning horse and war games together. His name had been Curly then. It had been changed, Harper learned, to that of his father and his father's father, after a great battle where young Curly rode his pony among an enemy warrior force according to a vision that had told him how to gain honor. He had been wounded, but had driven the enemy from their

stand upon a hill of rocks and had gained a scalp. His father had then announced with pride that his son, Curly, would now take the name Crazy Horse and become a great warrior.

Harper had learned this and much more from seeing Spotted Tail of the Brulé again after the close of the Fort Laramie peace conference. He had learned how determined Red Cloud was to stop the wagon people and keep the *Wasicun* from ruining the buffalo grasslands. Though it was true that Red Cloud had once wanted peace and had gone as far as to kill the horses of a war party getting ready for a raid, he was now fed up with what was happening and angered deeply that the Bluecoats considered his people to be like children. He would never again try to stop young warriors from killing wagon people and driving off their livestock. He would lead them. Though he had counted over forty winters, he would again go on the path of war, and young men like Crazy Horse would be given the greatest of support.

Carrington realized that the greatest concentration of Sioux would likely be north along the mountains, and that the fighting would become the most intense there. For this reason he had detached Captain Fetterman with the troops he had left at Fort Reno. He hoped the hot-headed young commander would learn more respect for his superiors there, under officers used to working with the galvanized Yankees brought out from the Yankee prison camps during the war. They were going back down to Fort Laramie and Carrington said silent prayers that Fetterman would be sent with them.

All the various divisions of the Sioux and the Cheyenne nations were now well aware of Carrington's march into the Powder River country. They knew him as the Little White Chief and considered him to be doing something he did not really understand. Each time they met with him, they heard him say he did not want war or fighting but only to establish Bluecoat posts from which he could watch the wagon people pass by and hear that they were traveling safely through

these lands. But they would not travel safely; they would be killed and their livestock driven away. They would wish they had never heard of the soft *Wasicun* metal called gold, which made them sick in the head. Carrington seemed not to understand that the Indians did not want their lands ruined so that the wagon people could be happy. The Little White Chief should leave the country or sing his death song.

Harper had prepared himself for war as well. In the sutler's store at Fort Reno he had traded his buckskin leggings for a Colt Dragoon pistol that had been converted for metallic cartridges and a belt to hold it with 50 rounds of ammunition. He had torn the sleeves from his blue coat, and on its back had painted the hook-beaked head and long talons of the red-tailed hawk, the zig-zag of a lightning bolt, and the open hand print of victory in hand-to-hand fighting. Harper's power was remembered among the Oglala and Bridger told Carrington to think of it as establishing authority rather than defacing a uniform.

To Harper it did not matter what any of the commanders thought; he was preparing himself to meet an enemy who had once been his family. He was not fighting for this Bluecoat army, but for his own honor. To them he now looked more like the warriors in the hills than a cavalry soldier assigned to help Bridger scout and interact with the Indians. They all avoided him, and he had explicit orders from Carrington to stay away from the women on the expedition because they were afraid of him.

The warriors on the hills began to taunt him and try to make him think he was weak for having become a Bluecoat. He was told he belonged among their weak women and could not be a man to a true woman of the Indian peoples. This brought back memories of Snow Fawn and Fox Boy and made Harper even more anxious for the fighting to begin. They still feared him as a warrior and it would mean honor to anyone who even touched him in battle. Though he would be fighting against those he once fought beside, he had only

to think of that day when he was ransomed for horses and he was ready to meet any of them. Let the drums of war sound.

Carrington had studied the length of the upper valley for some days before he stepped onto a small plateau of land that rested between the two branches of Piney Creek and announced that he wanted Fort Kearny placed there. Harper listened while Bridger argued with Carrington that better locations existed out a ways where the hills flattened some and the cover to hide warring Indians was more scattered. Carrington studied the blueprints and nodded; but when Bridger was finished speaking, he ordered men to hitch up horses to the mowing machines and clear the grass so that the survey could get started.

Harper was ordered to become the armed escort for the wood trains that ran regularly from the sawmills that had been established along the timbered lower slopes of the mountains. He was given a breech-loading Springfield and was told that in case of attack, the wagons were to be circled and there was to be no shooting unless absolutely necessary. There were less than ten rounds per man and only under life or death circumstances could it be expended. Harper gave the rifle back and fashioned himself a bow and some crude arrows. He was sure he would stand a better chance with his choice of weapons.

What the men were calling Phil Kearny was now under construction, with Carrington standing aside nodding and crossing his arms at regular intervals. His pride. He would convince his enemies in Washington and elsewhere that he was indeed the man for this job. Everything would fit nicely everywhere, in every detail. A nearby knoll received a flagpole and the title Pilot Hill, from which sentinels could signal the appearance of wagon trains and columns of blue passing along the Bozeman Road beneath the hill and in front of the fort. To make the stop at Phil Kearny even more of a traveler's pleasurable escapade, the name Sullivant Hills

appeared on a map, along with Lodge Trail Ridge. Nifty names and exotic titles would add to the glamor of this mountain fort, which seemed to Harper was becoming more of a show for the *Wasicun* wagon people than an actual bastion.

The men were kept busy building and no one took the time to learn how to fight. Most of the force were young, new recruits, many of whom had never seen any fighting. Since the regiment was comprised of infantry, those who had been given horses had never really learned to ride that well and could never be expected to fight on the run. Harper was surprised that the warriors watching had not been able to see this during the journey from Fort Laramie. Perhaps they had but were only intending to fight when the odds were even more in their favor.

When the Cheyenne came to the fort wanting to talk peace, Harper was assigned to interpret with Bridger. Under their leaders Two Moon, Black Horse, and Dull Knife, a small party of warriors came onto the fort grounds and received presents of tobacco, sugar, and flour, and the council pipe was lit. Their eyes traveled over everything, seeing the strengths and weaknesses of the post. While Two Moon and Black Horse did most of the talking, Dull Knife sat silent and took mental notes of what was happening all around these hills. Maybe they had come to actually talk of peace; but if it came time for them to fight, they would know the strong and weak points of this fort.

Carrington ordered the marching band to play and the Cheyenne nodded their appreciation. Then Carrington had one of the big field cannons fired to show the Bluecoat strength. The Cheyenne held their hands over their mouths in amazement as the shell exploded against a hillside above the fort. This showed the medicine of these big guns was powerful and many warriors could die from a single blast. By now they were not confused by the Bluecoat habit of mixing music and gaiety with threats of violence; this was common

and only showed they could not separate happiness from sadness. They could see there was a light in Carrington's eyes that meant he thought he had them under control now. The Little White Chief did not know the Indian people and was easy to fool.

"It shoots twice," Black Horse said as he pointed to the field cannon. "The Little White Chief shoots it once and the Little White Chief's Great Spirit fires it once more for his white children."

Carrington nodded and gave each of the leaders a piece of paper that stated they had agreed to peace with those *Wasicun* people who wished to cross these lands in their white wagons. The Cheyennes nodded and climbed back upon their ponies. When they were gone, Bridger confided to Harper that the field cannon should never have been fired. It meant Carrington had shown them his greatest strength, which should have been kept a secret.

"Sooner or later those Cheyenne will be in the fight as thick as the Sioux," Bridger told Harper. "The Sioux will get them into it, and then they'll all know better than to storm this place straight out. They'll just pick at the wood trains and everybody who goes out. Pick and pick and pick until it drives everybody crazy. Then somebody will go out after them and they'll chop them to bits and spread the chunks for the wolves."

Carrington later sent Bridger north with a commander and two companies of troops to build another fort where the Bozeman Trail crossed the Bighorn River. Fort C.F. Smith was sorely needed; wagons passing through that stretch were being attacked on a regular basis and there were getting to be a lot of gravesites along the road. Red Cloud's plan to fight in many places at once was going well and the war drums had now begun to sound continually.

With Bridger gone, Harper became like a starling in a flock of bluebirds. He could relate to nobody and they

thought of him as more like the warriors who now came at them almost daily, stealing the horses and mules and killing whenever they could strike quickly and be gone. Since the wood trains were constantly being harassed, troopers accompanied them now. None of the warriors ever came close enough for Harper to fight, but they taunted him, calling him a child for not leaving the cover of his Bluecoat friends.

An inspector general named Hazen showed up with supplies and re-enforcements, lifting the spirits of the men and making Carrington cautious. Hazen began by telling Carrington that he was building the finest stockade since the Hudson Bay Company's fur trading posts of early British America. He then mentioned that his priorities in construction within the fort would include the barracks and equipment sheds before he worried about his own private house. The regimental band had been building a standout two-story house for Carrington and his wife while the regular ranks slept in tents. Hazen also reminded Carrington that Harper's dress was not befitting an enlisted man in the U.S. Army and that disciplinary action should be considered. When Hazen left, Carrington considered himself to have lost ground as a commander in the eyes of his superiors. They liked the way he built forts, but not the way he handled men.

Carrington knew better than to tell Harper to conform to dress code. He did not even consider it. Without Harper the wood trains from the fort would have met with certain disaster. He was aware that his soldiers all considered him dangerous and unpredictable. Once when a wagon train had come through, one of the enlisted men found some whiskey and wanted Harper to do a war dance. Harper had promptly cut off both the man's ears. There was outrage when the drunken soldier had received his medical attention in the guardhouse while Harper escorted another wood train out. Carrington might not know much about Indians, but he knew Harper would have killed the drunken soldier if they had been placed in a cell together.

Late that fall Captain Fetterman arrived and Carrington threw his hat against the ground when he heard that Fetterman wanted to take Harper as a scout and go after Indian villages. For two weeks they wrangled until the flag on Pilot Hill signaled another column of soldiers approaching and Colonel Roland Deals led his command to the gates of Phil Kearny. It would do no good for Carrington to rant and rave about insubordination this time: Deals had a copy of orders directed to him personally, and signed by a high official in Washington.

"I didn't figure to ever see the likes o' you again, lad," O'Leary said as he greeted Harper. "It's good to see you, but I wished it weren't here and with Cornhead Deals in command. There's to be trouble for certain."

Harper thought back to the peace council at Fort Laramie early that summer and remembered Deals' promise about finding him and using him as his scout for a mission he was planning. With the connections Deals had in Washington, he could go anywhere and do anything he wanted. Apparently, he thought he could use O'Leary for something that Harper had trouble understanding.

"The word here was that all the galvanized Yankees were headed down to Laramie," Harper said to O'Leary. "I thought you would be out of this army by now and figured you would be with one of these wagon trains moving through here."

O'Leary pointed to the stripes sewed to his uniform jacket. "I was told my enlistment was not up and Deals gave me a sergeants' rank to come along with him up here. I didn't know what the hell was goin' on until he started askin' me questions about you. Somehow he knew that you and I are friends, and I somehow figure he wants to use me for some reason."

Carrington had taken Deals and Fetterman inside his office and their shouting was plainly heard. For the first time ever, Fetterman was arguing in Carrington's behalf. It was

well known among the ranking officers that whoever led the first successful major attack against the Sioux would be widely recognized and have an excellent chance for promotion. Fetterman and Deals were vying for that opportunity and Deals clearly had the upper hand.

"Deals wants to kill Indians," Harper said to O'Leary. "He won't make anyone believe otherwise. But what are these orders he keeps waving in Carrington's face?"

"He calls it the Sampson Mission," O'Leary answered. "Word has it some big politician in the East locked horns with his wife and she left him. To get clear away from him, she took their son and joined a train of wagons headed to Virginia City. It seems she has a sister who's husband struck it rich up there. Just before Lake DeSmet down here the Sioux came down on them and burned some wagons. Her boy, the politician's son, was down by the river with some other boys and they all got taken off by the warriors. For sure his name ain't Sampson, but Deals put a name tag on this whole thing just the same."

It was apparent that Deals could look forward to great rewards if this mission were to prove successful. O'Leary's part would be to give Harper support and encourage him to do his best to make things work out well for all. Deals was a shrewd tactician and his initial discussion with Harper was an attempt to smooth things over and to make it appear as if he held no grudge for past hostilities between them. He was careful to catch Harper at a time when drills were being conducted so that they could talk alone.

"I would like to wipe the slate clean," Deals told Harper. "In the past I have perhaps overlooked your qualities as a true gentleman. It is a rare man indeed who can adjust to a system such as this after being raised by savages, and emerge with the dignity you have. My congratulations to you."

"What do you want of me?"

"Well, I believe we can both gain a great deal by locating and rescuing this lost boy I am sure you have heard about by

now. You can certainly sympathize with the poor young fellow, having yourself been in such a predicament. I would like to have you arrange a meeting with Red Cloud so that we might learn the position of their villages, particularly the one in which the Sampson boy is being held."

"Do you know what he looks like or how old he is?"

Deals shrugged. "I understand he is about ten years old. Red hair. A lot of freckles."

"What if they won't give him up?"

"They will."

"What makes you so sure?"

Deals pointed to the livestock herds under careful guard. "We have brought a lot of good horses. I understand these Sioux and Cheyenne out here are very short on horses, and that they even eat them. How disgusting."

"The buffalo have been pushed out of here, so it's eat horses or starve."

Deals grunted. "I can understand your sympathy for them private Harper, and I believe it can only be considered natural for you to think in those terms. After all, your childhood was spent among them. But you must now realize that it is time you reached your real potential and used this opportunity to strike back at them for ruining your life."

"I do not want to go."

"Private Harper, you have no choice. Your name is on these orders." He waved the papers briskly at Harper. "If you disobey, I have the authority to have you court-martialed. And believe me, you insubordinate savage-lover, I will exercise that authority with the greatest of pleasure. I want Red Cloud at this fort to talk within two days. Is that clear, private Harper? Within two days." His arm swept the hills. "He is out there and you know which one he is. There is no more to discuss." He turned and made his way toward the cavalry yard, swinging the orders around as he walked, whistling a tune.

*　　*　　*

Red Cloud brought nearly fifty of his warriors with him to council at Phil Kearny. Tobacco for the men and odds and ends for the women were presented before the council began. Red Cloud would not light the pipe, which Deals was happy about. It meant less time fooling around with formalities and more time to talk business. There was also no band performance and no shooting of the cannon. Red Cloud had not been asked to come and talk of peace. He had come only because Harper had signaled a warrior that a meeting was desired and there would be horses for him and his people if he attended.

With Red Cloud was Crazy Horse, who began the discussion.

"It is strange to meet you again this way," he said to Harper. "When we were boys we played war games together and now you wear the blue of those whom we hate. You wear it with the symbols of your power as a Bad Face warrior. Your heart is divided between two peoples."

"My heart is angry," Harper said. "I once loved all those in the Bad Face band of Oglala people, but I was turned out for horses. I was forced to become a Bluecoat, and I feel this is good. I can now fight the people who destroyed my life."

"So you like being a *Wasicun* and a Bluecoat? And you wish to fight with them so that they can take our hunting grounds and call them theirs?"

"Crazy Horse, you talk of things that are happening now, but I have spent seven winters of unhappiness since I last saw you. You have told me only that you find it strange to see me with the Bluecoats fighting against the people I once called my own; you have not yet called me brother."

"You are with the Bluecoats, and the Bluecoats are bad."

"There are good men among these Bluecoats, as there are among the Indian peoples. And there are those who are bad. Is this not the way of all life?"

Red Cloud, who had been listening intently, now spoke up. "You both have talked enough of something that cannot be

changed. A decision was made by the council seven winters past that we must now live with, be it good or bad. No one will blame a man for anger at what he thinks is wrong. And those who believe they are right will never back down. We have come at your request, Sun Hair. What does the new white chief with the strange hat come to these lands for?"

"He says you now hold a young *Wasicun* boy captive in your village, a boy with red hair who was taken during an attack on wagons that came into these lands. Do you have him?"

Red Cloud's face was without expression. He looked over at Deals for a time before he turned back to Harper.

"Does the new white chief wish to trade for the release of this *Wasicun* boy in the manner you were traded for seven winters past?"

Harper nodded. "Do you have him?"

"Let me talk with the others who have come with me," Red Cloud said, "to see if they wish to release him."

Red Cloud called his warriors aside while Harper asked him again if the boy was present in their village. Deals immediately began to hound Harper about what had been said and both Carrington and Fetterman made it plain that the talk was to include all of them at this point. Harper reminded the three of them that Red Cloud would leave at any time if he did not like the way the talks were going, leaving them all with no solution to the problem of the captive white boy. Also, since they were outside the fort, as agreed to by Carrington, the warriors waiting in force along the hills could come down and kill a lot of soldiers if Red Cloud suspected a trap of some sort. Red Cloud had taken no chances and had had everything arranged to suit him, including conference only with Harper until he was ready to include the Little White Chief and the new white chief with the strange hat.

Fetterman now had to be content to sit back and watch while Deals embarked on the mission that had been his dream since coming to this country. There was nothing he

could do but sit and fret and hope something drastic happened to Deals. Harper would ask Red Cloud again if the red-haired boy Deals had called Sampson was in their village, realizing Red Cloud would likely choose not to answer. It seemed apparent to Harper that Red Cloud and Deals understood one another very well without having exchanged a single word: they both wanted to kill one another.

CHAPTER 8

"The *Wasicun* boy is in our village on the Crazy Woman Fork. We will release him to the new chief if he has many horses, and also the many-shoots rifles with many of the bullets that go into them." Red Cloud stood in front of Harper with his hands folded across his chest. "You can tell this to both the new chief and the Little White Chief. Tell them I cannot wait long for an answer."

Harper told Carrington and Deals what Red Cloud had said, including the demand for the new Henry repeating rifles that many of the traders and freight drivers were carrying with them.

"He has no business asking for Henry rifles," Carrington said, throwing up his hands. "They haven't even been issued to *us* yet. How does he expect to get them when we don't have any?"

"Tell him you will give him some breech-loading Springfields," Harper suggested. "They don't shoot that far anyway."

"I can't justify giving him rifles of any kind," Carrington said.

Deals then broke in, addressing himself to Harper. "Tell them we will deliver the horses and other presents to his village. Tell him we will bring rifles, but that we have no new Henry repeaters."

"No!" Carrington blared. "That is crazy, Colonel Deals. Have them bring the boy here to the fort. They can receive their presents for him when they come with him."

Deals again produced the papers on which his orders were drawn. "These orders are specific, Colonel Carrington! I am

to search until I find the boy. That means everywhere, and anywhere I choose to do so!"

Carrington clenched his fists. "I don't give a damn about those orders! I am in command of this district and will not allow a crazy stunt such as this to take place!"

"Very well, Colonel Carrington," Deals backed off. "We shall have it your way, if that's what you want. But you will receive word in a very short time that you have exercised your command here at Phil Kearny in direct violation of this document, and it will cost you your position here, sir. You know very well how many men there are above you who are sorry they agreed to your assignment here in the first place. This is all it will take to have you removed."

"I am not telling you to abort your mission, Colonel," Carrington stated quickly. "I am only suggesting that you consider all the details in these negotiations with Red Cloud. Why go out to his village when your men are outnumbered ten to one? Why take the chance of a disaster? Have the boy brought here."

"We have nothing to fear by going to their village," Deals assured Carrington. "I have a field cannon and I intend to borrow one of yours. They will not attack us."

Carrington blew out his breath. "As you wish, Colonel. But I will go on record as not recommending your actions."

"That is your privilege, Colonel," Deals grinned.

Harper then told Red Cloud that horses and other presents would be brought to their village on the Crazy Woman Fork, but that no rifles of any kind would be traded. Red Cloud merely nodded and called his warriors together to bid final goodbyes. It was obvious to Harper that Red Cloud did not care about the rifles, nor the horses either for that matter. He cared only about getting Bluecoat soldiers away from the fort. Red Cloud told Harper that they would have the boy ready to make the trade after the passing of three suns. "It is strange that you can adjust to life among these Bluecoats," he told Harper as he climbed on his pony. "And it is certain that you will die if you stay among them."

*   *   *

Deals forced Carrington into giving him a company of cavalry to fortify the other two companies he had brought with him. In addition, Deals demanded the loan of another field cannon to supplement the one he had brought from Fort Laramie. Carrington could do little more than fume over the situation; his hands were tied by a set of orders and a man who was going to try and take his job away from him one way or another.

Just before departure, Fetterman approached Harper and hissed, "Harper, you have double-crossed me. You were supposed to scout for *me* on a campaign against Red Cloud. Now you turn your back and go off to implement my own plan with your friend, Colonel Deals."

"My friend Deals?"

"Don't be coy with me, private Harper. Colonel Deals is the commander who got you out of the Sioux village seven years ago. You now plan to show how grateful you are by stealing my idea and giving it to him!"

"My name is on those orders. I've got to go whether I want to or not."

"I'm sure you had this whole thing arranged down at Fort Laramie during the peace conference. Colonel Deals included you so that you would be sure and get to go. Well, go then if you must. But remember, private, that I have an exceedingly long memory about things such as this. You can be assured that I will return this favor in good time." He turned without salute and walked stiffly back into the fort grounds.

O'Leary came up to Harper as Deals got the column lined up to move out and said with a wink, "You've got more friends than you know what to do with, lad. How is it you can make everyone so happy all at once like you do. Must be a gift, I'd say."

Harper made a mock salute to O'Leary. "Whatever you say, Sergeant O'Leary. But might I say, sir, that my troubles began when I first met you."

O'Leary laughed. "That door swings both ways, you white Injun son-of-a-bitch. But you do play a mighty good whistle, so I'll forgive you. Do you figure we're all bound to die?"

"There comes a time when we all must die," Harper said. "If it is not a quick and sudden death that happens when we least expect it, then it is a death that we can foresee for a time before it comes. Do you feel that we are headed for death?"

"Hell, I'm too scared to think about anything. I just want to know how you feel about it."

"Red Cloud and Crazy Horse want to kill us all," Harper said. "But they will not risk the women and children of their people. That is what you must remember."

Harper and O'Leary joined Deals at the head of the column and the long line of blue began to twist itself away from the fort through the rolling foothills. Now that the snow moons were coming, the land was preparing for the cold. The grass had turned a light gold and the trees and shrubs were releasing their last hold on the leaves that had been so green during the march up the Bozeman Trail. The once multicolored wildflowers were now twisted stalks, their roots hiding in the dark soil, waiting for a new spring to trigger them into the renewed vigor of life.

The wind seemed sad, the day lonely as a heavy bank of clouds pushed over the jagged top of Cloud Peak and a mist of rain began to fall. The soldiers talked and laughed in the ranks as Harper led them toward the Crazy Woman Fork of the Powder River, few of them aware of Deals's plans. They were little more than youngsters eager to write letters back home of their times in Red Cloud's country. Few of them knew how to shoot well and even fewer had ever shot at another man. They had never heard an Oglala war cry nor the sound of hatchets cleaving muscle and bone. Only those of the company from Phil Kearny who had been forced to join this command knew anything of what they were riding toward, and most of them had only chased fleeing Indians or escaped attacking ones. Those few who had seen a friend fall

or looked into the painted face of hate were riding with their muscles tight and their heads turning all about them. Harper knew that by the time they reached the Oglala village on Crazy Woman Fork, these few men would have spread the fear and apprehension throughout the ranks. There would be a real sense of what this mission was truly about and the laughing would then turn to praying.

Harper knew this camping place well, for it had been a favorite fall hunting area for the Bad Faces when he was a boy. It was early in the morning and smoke curled from the tops of a great many lodges below. Harper was grooming the mud and tangled hair from the trade horses and preparing them for the trip down to council with Red Cloud. He made their coats shine and plaited bright strips of cloth into their manes and tails. They had to look good if Red Cloud and the other leaders were to think them worthy of trade.

As he worked, Harper studied the village below and the country for miles around in every direction. The village was on a flat overlooking Crazy Woman Fork but a small stream twisted down from just above the village. There were no women and children in evidence which was to be expected. Dogs roamed about and barked up at the soldiers, some of them moving in and out of the small draw above the village. Deals came over to Harper then and curled his lips.

"You have brought me where I wanted to come. I didn't think you would actually do it."

"I told Red Cloud I was coming here with you and the others to trade for a red-haired boy. If I was to have taken you any other place, we would have been much easier to kill."

"What do you mean?"

"The time for games is over, Deals. You came here to wipe out this village. Red Cloud knows that. Do you take him for a fool?"

"I want the boy first," Deals said. "Do you understand? I must have that boy."

"Do you really think there is a red-haired boy here?"
Deal's eyes widened. "There had better be."

"And what if there isn't? Will your friend in Washington have your stripes?"

Deals began to get panicky. "Forget those horses. I intend to proceed with my plan of action immediately."

"They haven't signaled that they are ready to council yet."

"To hell with the signal! I am going to divide the command, half on either side of the village. I will then have the cannons brought up to the middle and trained on the village itself. You and I will then speak with Red Cloud. He damn well better have that boy."

"We aren't going down there just yet," Harper said sternly. "I know these people and you brought me along to assist you. I'll tell you when the time is right."

"I have had quite enough of you, Harper," Deals said through his teeth. "I don't need you now anyway." He pulled his pistol and trained it on Harper. "I want you to place both your gun and your knife upon the ground at your feet."

Harper did what he was told without question. Deals's eyes were wild and filled with hate. It seemed to matter little to him that shots might alarm the warriors in Red Cloud's village. Harper tried to point out to Deals that there were scouts stationed around watching them and that warriors were gathering in the village below. Red Cloud would be ready to talk at any moment.

"I have a surprise for you, Harper," Deals went on, ignoring anything Harper was trying to tell him. He yelled back to the men, "Sergeant O'Leary, report to me here on the double."

O'Leary came over, worry etched deep into his face.

"Sergeant O'Leary, draw your pistol please. I want it known to you that private Harper has conducted himself in such a manner as to warrant execution." Deals then quickly trained his pistol on O'Leary. "Shoot him! Kill him or I will kill you!"

O'Leary began to laugh. "As you wish, sir." O'Leary cocked his pistol and trained it on Deals. "At the count of three we both fire. What do you say to that, sir? One . . ."

"Wait!" Deals blurted. He knew if he took his pistol off O'Leary, he would be shot immediately. But now that Harper had picked up his pistol and knife, he didn't know what to do.

"I think I'll end it," O'Leary said. "No matter what, I think I'll just pull this trigger."

"Don't, O'Leary," Harper said. "He's not worth it. This whole force is going to get cut to bits very soon if we don't act right now."

O'Leary and Deals both lowered their pistols. Below, Red Cloud was painting his horse for war. With him was a number of prominant warriors. Crazy Horse was not among them but Harper knew exactly what they had planned.

"You have two choices, Deals," Harper said. "You can direct your men according to what I tell you, or you can watch O'Leary and me ride out of here now and hope Red Cloud's warriors don't catch us and butcher us."

"What do you want to do?" Deals nodded, still stunned by what had just taken place. He was like a puppet now, his hands shaking and his voice trembling, willing to follow Harper's every wish. He had been planning to have O'Leary kill Harper and had never thought that O'Leary might give up his own life rather than kill a friend. Now the possibility of dying at the hands of the Oglala Sioux seemed very real to him.

Harper divided the column in two and sent Deals with half of the men onto a ridge above the small stream that wound its way down to the Crazy Woman Fork. He then led the other half of the force along a hillside above the village and down into the bottom of a small draw. The cannons were aimed at the heavy stand of trees and brush along the stream bottom. Dogs barked and snapped all around them, but no noise came from the heavy brush cover. Children were

trained as infants to make no sound when an enemy was near, even in the face of death, nor would they run unless given the signal by the warriors. Deals and the remainder of the force were lined along the ridge above them. Though warriors screamed and yelled and ran their horses across the bottom as decoys, Harper stood firm and waited. Before he had even finished preparing himself to fight, Red Cloud appeared on his pony at the bottom of the draw and signaled for council.

"The trick is on you this day," Harper told him as they met. "You have an empty village with smoke coming from every lodge. But the camp dogs want to be with the children and they travel this small draw."

"No, Sun Hair," Red Cloud came back, "the trick is on you. It is true that the women and children are hidden there in the cover along the stream and it is true that I have prepared my warriors to fight this day, but a boy awaits in a lodge below. He is to be ransomed for horses, as we agreed."

"You would not answer me about the boy at the fort called Phil Kearny," Harper said. "You would not answer yes or no. I did not believe there is a boy."

"There is a boy," Red Cloud said. "Do you wish to fight or trade?"

Warriors were now taking their positions along the slope of the hill between Deals and his troops at the top and the hidden women and children at the bottom. Harper knew that if fighting started these warriors would be far braver than if there were no women and children to defend. There was also no real way to decide what Deals would do under this kind of pressure. He seemed jittery and insecure, but he might order an attack at any time.

Harper rode up the hill and told Deals that Red Cloud did not want to fight, only to trade for the boy who was in one of the lodges on the bottom. Deals seemed to be trying to push himself away from the reality of what he had got himself into, trying to decide whether to fight or run.

"Deals, you must remain calm," Harper said to him. "These warriors can just sit on their ponies like this for the rest of the day if they have to. There will be no fighting unless you or Red Cloud start it. They have their women and children to think about and believe me if anything starts, we'll all be cut to pieces."

Deals was breathing heavily, his eyes open wide. "Don't leave me," he said. "Don't leave. They won't do anything as long as you are here."

"They will not do anything if I leave," Harper assured him. "This is not a time for glory among them. If their trick had succeeded, we would have all died before this. Now there are none among them who want a fight."

"Don't leave me."

"I will go down into the village and bring the boy back up here with me. Nothing will happen while I am gone. Then the boy can go back to his father in the East and your mission will have been a success. That is the way it will work. Do you understand me, Deals?"

Deals nodded and gripped the reins tightly in his hands. His horse jerked its head from the pressure against its mouth.

"Just stay put and relax," Harper said again. "I will come back soon with the boy."

Harper rode back down and told O'Leary that the most important thing was to keep at least six men stationed around the field cannon with another six at the ready. The warriors were well aware of the damage these big guns could do at close quarters and would certainly not chance having them fired at their women and children.

"Take me to the boy," Harper told Red Cloud.

"Have the big guns turned around," Red Cloud said.

"When I come back with the boy and you have the trade horses. Not until. Then we will leave with the big guns."

Red Cloud took Harper to a lodge near the center of the village. A warrior standing guard near the doorflap moved

aside when Red Cloud and Harper got down from their horses. Red Cloud folded his arms and looked hard at Harper.

"Do you think you are like the others who wear the blue of the *Wasicun* warrior?"

"No," Harper answered.

Red Cloud pointed to the doorflap of the lodge. "We shall soon see."

Harper entered the lodge and looked into the eyes of Snow Fawn and Fox Boy. She had lost none of her beauty, that spark of deep pride still bright in her eyes. Fox Boy was young and sleek and strong. His eyes told that he was looking at a man who was said to be his father, but who wore the blue of the enemy. When Harper finally spoke it was to try and once again rearrange his feelings.

"I thought you both had died at Sand Creek, the Little Dried River."

"Many died there," Snow Fawn said. "There were those of us who escaped, but our scars are in the mind and not on the body. Black Kettle lost his honor that day, because he did not want to fight."

"What of Elk-Dancing-at-Night, your husband?"

"His life ended there. His brother and two sisters were killed also. I came back to the Bad Faces to live with my brother's family."

Fox Boy sat silent and watched his father. Harper could read in his eyes the same expression of frustration and anger he himself had felt that day the Bluecoats had come to take him away. Snow Fawn's eyes were equally as disturbed.

"Where is the red-haired *Wasicun* boy?" Harper asked her.

"I have heard of no such boy. I was told that I must use Fox Boy so that many Bluecoats could be tricked and killed. That is all I know."

Harper could feel the flow of anger and frustration that pushed out from her and twisted itself around him as if it were a serpent trying to squeeze the life from his body. She

had had no choice but to go along with the decision made by Red Cloud and the other warriors of the council, to place herself and Fox Boy in great danger so that the hated Bluecoats could be surrounded and killed. She could sense now that things had not gone as Red Cloud had planned.

"You know by now that I took the Bluecoat soldiers and had them aim their guns at the women and children hiding along the stream above the village," Harper told her. "I did not wish to die this day and I knew that Red Cloud would not want to fight if he could not lure us into a trap."

"You are a dog!" Snow Fawn spat. "You wear the colors of those who want us all to die and be gone from these lands."

"I was made to wear these colors," Harper tried to explain, "and until this day I was glad for it. There has been much anger in my heart for being sent away from this band and I have waited for the day when I could make these people wish they had never traded me for horses. Now the day I have waited for is here and I find you and Fox Boy. For me life has been hard to understand."

"Each of us has the free will to make our own decisions," Snow Fawn said, her voice still hard. "Many winters ago you decided you wished to take the daughter of Man-Afraid-of-His-Horses for your wife. She did not want this, so you had no wife then the lying Bluecoats told Red Cloud and my people that the captives must be returned to gain peace. You had been a captive and you were returned. Now you want to blame the Oglala people for this."

"Who would you have blamed if it had been someone else but me who came to the village this day and Fox Boy had been brought to the Bluecoats and perhaps killed when the fighting started? Would you not have blamed Red Cloud and the others in the council who made the decision to use you both to kill the Bluecoats?"

"I would not have had the same kind of anger as you," Snow Fawn answered. "You are more angry with yourself than with anyone else, for you made the wrong decision

many winters past. Deep within, you know your troubles have been caused by what you did and not because of what others did to you. Red Cloud assured me that we would not be close to the fighting and that there was little chance of danger to us. I believe now that Red Cloud put us here only to test you. Fox Boy does not have red hair and does not look like a *Wasicun* boy. He is not even dressed like a *Wasicun* boy. No one would think he was a captive, not even if one were in these lands for the first time. I believe Red Cloud wants to see how angry you really are and if you have truly become a *Wasicun* and a Bluecoat."

Outside and from the distance came the music of a penny whistle. It was a lyrical, bouncy tune in the style that O'Leary had played seven winters past when Red Cloud and his warriors had looked down on the small wagon train by the Platte River.

"What is the strange music?" Snow Fawn asked.

Harper was able to grin. "There is one among the Bluecoats who has great medicine with the whistle. It is he who is playing so that there might be no fighting."

Harper went outside the lodge where he met Red Cloud again. Red Cloud was looking up from the village to where O'Leary was playing and dancing a jig on the flat between the cavalry and the cover along the stream where the women and children were hiding.

"It is the same old Bluecoat who played that day when you broke our medicine against the wagon people," Red Cloud said. "This is not a good omen. Does the old Bluecoat feel that the spirits are again with him?"

"Yes," Harper answered. "It would be good if the Bluecoats were allowed to leave with no fighting."

Red Cloud turned to face Harper. "You came to fight and take revenge against those of us who sent you away seven winters past. Does what you have seen in this lodge change your heart?"

"Fox Boy is of my blood," Harper said. "There is but one

choice for me to make this day, and that is to stay here while the Bluecoats leave. If you and the council decide that I am to die then, I will leave this life as a true warrior. If you decide that I can again be Oglala, as I once was, I will fight with you against the Bluecoats. There can be no other way."

O'Leary continued to play and dance on the flat above the village. He danced a circle around the two field cannons and worked his way along the edge of the trees and brush of the stream.

"Then you know why this lodge was prepared for you," Red Cloud said. "Your skin is of the *Wasicun* color and we all wished to know the true color of your heart. You have told me now that your heart is with the son you once fathered and I believe you. You were once an Oglala warrior and you were betrayed. That is in the past. You can again have honor among us if you wish to have it."

There was the sound of O'Leary's whistle up on the flat while Harper nodded to Red Cloud, and then the pounding of running horses drowned out the music. Deals had panicked and was leading his half of the command down from the ridge and away from the village as fast as he could. Those along the bottom then rushed past O'Leary on their horses and out across the stream in front of the village to join Deals and the others. O'Leary was left standing with his whistle while warriors began to whoop and surge past him after the soldiers. Those standing near the cannons were killed immediately, but none of the warriors came anywhere near O'Leary. His medicine was of a strange and wonderful kind. Not one of power, but a force of happiness. If he was killed, the spirits would look down with great disfavor.

Deals and his half of the command had a considerable head start on the warriors, but the other half on the bottom was quickly overtaken by the Oglala forces. Crazy Horse screamed his war cry as he worked his pony in next to a Bluecoat soldier and swung his war club repeatedly until the soldier fell. It was a running fight and the casualties on both

sides would not be high. Crazy Horse and the other warriors would strike whenever it appeared they could swoop in and not be shot by a carbine or a pistol. They gave up the chase as soon as they saw that the troops ahead with Deals had turned and were charging back toward them. Those few warriors who lay injured on the ground were picked up with war ropes and taken back to the village while the soldiers worked their horses to catch up with Deals and the others.

The Oglala women and children came out from hiding and began to strip and mutilate the dead soldiers around the two field cannon. O'Leary broke through a group of children who had gathered around to touch him and tried to stop them. Harper pulled him back and made him turn away.

"That is the way of Indian warfare," Harper explained. "You cannot stop them."

O'Leary was sick. "It ain't right. How can you let them cut those boys to pieces? Some of them ain't even dead yet."

"Do not interfere," Harper said again. "You will not die because of your medicine with the whistle. I will not die because I am again one of them."

O'Leary stared. "You plan to stay with them?"

Harper pointed back to the cluster of lodges on the bottom. "There was no red-haired boy for me to see down there. It was my son. Red Cloud took me to see my son, whom I have told you about. He and his mother did not die at Sand Creek. I must stay with him now. He is my family."

O'Leary nodded. "You don't think they will want to kill me and cut me up like the others?"

"No. They will allow you to leave. Maybe you can find a wagon train bound for the gold fields, like you always wanted."

"I figure maybe I can in time," O'Leary nodded. "Now I've got no choice but to find a fort in one hell of a hurry. I didn't figure this whistle would ever save my life and I don't plan to

rely on it none the next time I meet a bunch of warrin'
Injuns."

"Go down to Fort Reno," Harper suggested. "Phil Kearny
will burn some day. There will be many attacks against it as
time goes on."

"I guess I can understand what you're doin'," O'Leary said,
"since your son is alive and all. And I guess you never did
really fit in with the rest of those soldiers. But it seems I don't
get a lot of time to be around you before your plans change."

"I will remember you always," Harper told O'Leary. "And
I will not say goodbye, for life will bring us together again, I
am sure. I will only say goodbye for now."

O'Leary rode his horse over the ridge and across the
pattern of rolling hills, avoiding the bottom where women
and warriors alike were spread up and down the course of
the Crazy Woman Fork, using their knives and hatchets and
clubs on the fallen Bluecoats. Harper watched him disappear
in the distance, thinking that if Deals had not run away with
his half of the command there would likely have been no
fighting at all. But for O'Leary the fighting had been his
salvation: Deals would surely have had him court-martialed
for disobeying his orders. As it was, O'Leary had whistled his
way past certain death and now rode away with the daze of
what had happened so very quickly still left in his eyes.

Harper turned back again to see Snow Fawn and Fox Boy
watching him from the edge of the village. They turned
away and went back into their lodge, closing the doorflap
behind them. Harper had come back to his true people, but
it would be hard for them to accept him.

Part Three

It is good to have an end to journey towards;
but it is the journey that matters, in the end.

Ursula K. Le Guin

CHAPTER 9

He walks among the Bad Face band of Oglala people, a man who was once given back to his own people and has returned to live again with his adopted family. It is said once again that he might some day become a legend, as is the one called Red Cloud, the main leader among these people. He was once said to be strong and flashy in battle, this man whose hair is the light gold color of the morning sun on sandstone and whose eyes are the color of the evening sky. The one called Sun Hair wishes many honors once again.

But he walks now in a time when the Oglala people have seen much change and have suffered many wrongs at the hands of the Bluecoats who now live in these lands in great numbers. They have killed many of the Oglala people and ride now alongside the white-topped wagons that come through the buffalo grasslands in endless lines. These Bluecoats care only to drive the Oglala and the other Indian peoples from these lands forever so that the Wasicun can have it all for themselves. There can never be peace in these lands as long as the Bluecoats live in their forts and the Wasicun travel through in their white-topped wagons. Now the wagon people are dying along their road in great numbers and the Bluecoats are angry. There has been much fighting. It seems the fighting will continue forever.

The buffalo are mostly driven from these lands now. The peoples of the Sioux, Cheyenne, and the Arapaho see each coming of the cold moons take away the few that now remain among the old and the very young. The anger is now rage and there are no more tears left to fall. Nothing, it seems, can be done to stop this, and the elders still shake their heads and say that their dreams tell them to make peace, that it is better to try and live with the change.

The leaders of the many bands of the tribes are now divided. Some

119

listen to their elders and talk to the leaders of the Bluecoats to try and make peace, while others fight until they die. More papers are drawn up by the Bluecoats, but no one will ever again believe any of the promises . . .

Harper danced with the other warriors preparing for the big fight against the Bluecoats at Phil Kearny. He would now show that his heart was truly Oglala and not still among the *Wasicun*. He had been invited to live with a warrior named Bear Foot and his family, who was the younger brother of the man who had once been Harper's adopted father. What Spotted Tail of the Brulé had told him back at Fort Laramie was true: Standing Bull, his adopted father, had died fighting the Bluecoats led by the white chief Connor, who they called Star Chief. His adopted mother had died the winter past of the *Wasicun* coughing sickness. Harper had been an only child, even though Standing Bull had taken a younger wife who was now remarried. Now Harper was alone and he would again have to build his honor in the eyes of the Oglala people.

Snow Fawn and Fox Boy both watched the dancing, having taken their places in the outer circle while the men danced and pushed lances and knives into scalps placed on poles. There were few Bluecoat scalps among them. Most Bluecoats were not worthy of the honor and only those who showed great courage had hair that was strong and powerful.

Harper danced for Snow Fawn and Fox Boy more than he did any of the others. Since being taken in by the band he had been unable to speak much to Snow Fawn, for she did not want to be around him. While he had been making himself a war shield and arrows to fit his bow, he had made Fox Boy a small skinning knife. Fox Boy had smiled but still felt uneasy about his father. Harper hoped to show them that he truly wanted to be an Oglala Bad Face warrior again by taking part in the fighting against the Bluecoats. If he

gained honor during the fighting, it would prove to Snow Fawn that he wanted to stay with the band. Maybe she would then understand that he thought a great deal of her.

The first of the snows had already come and the war party moved quickly through the hills of patched white and up the Valley of Prairie Dogs. The Oglalas were joined by the Hunkpapas, the Minniconjous, and some Brulé and Blue Cloud warriors. The northern Cheyennes had also joined, for now was the time to bring the Little White Chief out of the fort and kill him and all of his Bluecoat soldiers. Harper felt good about what he was doing. Since leaving the soldiers to rejoin the Bad Face band, he had once again learned what it was like to be truly free and away from the demeaning *Wasicun* way of life. The only person who thought like him at all was O'Leary, now probably in the gold fields of Montana. It would be good to push the Bluecoats out so that the hunting grounds once again teemed with great herds of buffalo and the wagons never again made deep tracks through the grasslands.

Along the Peno Creek one of the Special Ones, a man-woman who lived among them, told of a dream in which many Bluecoats died in battle. The Special One then rode out into the cold wind with a special medicine blanket and performed a sacred ceremony he had learned in a dream. He returned to tell with dazed eyes that he had seen more dead Bluecoats along the bottom than could be counted many times on the fingers of both hands. The cold wind did not drown out the cries and yells that rose from the many mounted warriors who now knew that their own medicine would be strong. This would be the beginning of the hard fighting to drive the Bluecoats from the land.

Harper had been ready for this battle ever since his first days back with the Oglala, during which time he had gone out from the village to fast and regain the medicine of his spirit helper, the red-tailed hawk. His quest for medicine had been successful and he had returned after seeing the large

bird of prey circling the valley. He had been hailed as once again strong, for he had found a lost fingerbone necklace that had been made from the trigger fingers of many Bluecoat soldiers killed in the fighting over the many winters since they had first come to these lands. Harper wore this necklace now as part of his own power and he would soon show all those warriors who doubted him that he truely hated the Bluecoats.

There had been a few days of fighting, before this special day, when warriors had attacked the wood trains that left the fort each day and had brought many Bluecoats out from the fort, among them Fetterman and the Little White Chief, Carrington. Harper had not seen Deals among them and was sure that Deals had gone back to Fort Laramie for a time. As this special day of fighting dawned, Harper wished Deals was at Phil Kearny so that he might taste the sharp point of an arrow, or feel the burning furrow left inside him from the lead and powder of Harper's Colt Dragoon. Many of the Bluecoats would fall it was certain, for the Special One had dreamed this and had come from the little valley of Peno Creek with his hands showing many dead.

The battle plan was one of ambush that the Bluecoats had fallen for at other times. Harper was to be tested and was to go with Crazy Horse and a number of other warriors to act as decoys in luring the soldiers into ambush. Harper considered himself lucky: many wished to go with Crazy Horse and gain honor, for their lives would be in great danger. As the first flash of light appeared in the cold blue sky to the east, Harper spoke through breath that clouded from his mouth and told Crazy Horse he would wager two ponies that he could kill a Bluecoat before Crazy Horse could. Crazy Horse laughed and accepted the wager. This would be very dangerous and the winner would gain great honor.

The warriors were divided into three groups. A large force went with the warrior Hump to attack the wood train as it went to the base of the mountains, while the second group

took its position in the grass and brush in the draws on both sides of Peno Creek, where its head met Lodge Trail Ridge. Harper and the other decoys in the third group followed Crazy Horse to where the Bozeman Trail crossed the waters of Big Piney, just below the fort. The three groups were all spread apart, Harper sitting hidden among the cottonwoods with Crazy Horse and the others as the sun climbed into the morning sky.

Distant shots finally came from where Hump's warriors had surrounded the wood train. Harper watched the flag on Pilot Hill go up and saw the gates of Fort Phil Kearny open, spilling Bluecoat infantry as well as cavalry out across the frozen ground. Harper recognized their commander: Fetterman was yelling and waving his long sabre as he kicked his horse into a run.

Harper followed Crazy Horse and the other warriors out of the cover. Crazy Horse sang a war song and waved a blanket to divert the attention of the soldiers as they came up from the fort. A field cannon at the fort sounded and a ball exploded overhead as it crashed through the trees along the creek. Two warriors fell from their horses and two others turned their horses to go back and pick them up, while Harper and the rest of the decoy party began to shout insults at the oncoming Bluecoats. Instead of heading directly for the wood train, Fetterman turned his men toward the northwest and Lodge Trail Ridge. Hump had signaled to his warriors and they were circling back from the wood train and into the cover of the hills. It seemed to Harper that Fetterman intended to find and kill Indians this day, no matter where he had to go to do it.

Crazy Horse got down from his pony and checked its hooves, looking back toward the Bluecoats. Harper and the other warriors had by now got down from their ponies and were taking their time as they worked their way along the ridge. The sun was nearly overhead by now and there was no sign of Hump's warriors anywhere. Fetterman was looking

up at the warriors and it was plain that he had recognized Harper among them. He pointed Harper out to others in his command and all began returning the obscene gestures the warriors were making at them. Crazy Horse talked with the warriors, laughing and pointing down toward Fetterman and the other Bluecoats in his command. The infantry had now caught up with the cavalry and both groups were waiting for Fetterman to tell them what to do. Crazy Horse came over to Harper and told him to have two ponies ready for him when they returned to the village. Then he walked a ways up the ridge and built a fire.

Fetterman and his command started up the ridge, firing as they came. They would stop and ram the long rods down their Springfield muzzle-loaders before each shot. The balls came closer and closer to the warriors, the Bluecoats becoming braver and braver. Among them were two frontiersmen who had apparently been at the fort and had joined Fetterman for the adventure of killing Indians. One of them was making sign talk up to Harper, who read it through his spy glass.

"Colonel Fetterman says that you led Colonel Deals into a trap on the Crazy Woman Fork. He wants you to know that he will take your scalp and present it personally to Colonel Deals before the end of the year."

Harper then made sign back down for them to read while Fetterman watched through his own spy glass.

"Deals and Fetterman are both cowards, and it is difficult to say which one is worse. Neither of them are fit to drink the piss of an Indian warrior, though I have seen Fetterman do it many times." The laughter of Crazy Horse and the warriors with him carried down with the sign.

Fetterman drew his sabre again and gave the command to charge. Crazy Horse ordered the warriors over the top, where they scrambled back onto their ponies and scattered along the bottom of Peno Creek.

Fetterman reached the top of Lodge Trail Ridge and

began to ride his horse back and forth, shouting down to Harper that he was a coward and should come and fight. Harper and a few of the warriors circled their ponies around and began to advance on Fetterman and his command. The two frontiersmen came out in front with Fetterman and Harper could see that they had the new repeating Spencer rifles that Carrington had been wanting for so long. Again Harper had to laugh: the freight wagons and emigrant trains were still better armed than the military.

Crazy Horse had positioned himself on the other side of a draw at the head of Peno Creek, across from where Harper was now charging his pony toward Fetterman and the two frontiersmen. Harper clung to the side of his pony, away from the line of fire, and rode the horse in a zig-zag fashion as he came. From years of chasing buffalo, the squat pony was able to turn quickly and without losing speed, was nearly in front of the startled Fetterman when a soldier came from the ranks and urged his horse toward Harper's oncoming pony.

Harper's arrow drove through the soldier's stomach and he lurched forward off his horse while Harper wheeled his pony around and down toward the bottom of Peno Creek. The frontiersmen were reloading their seven-shot repeaters and cursing. They had both emptied their rifles and had not even come close to the horse, let alone Harper.

Now Fetterman was leading his troops in a line down one of the forks of Peno Creek after Harper and the other decoy warriors, who still waited in the bottom on their ponies. Crazy Horse had come from the other side to join them, holding two fingers up for Harper to see as he rode. Fetterman and his soldiers were yelling since it appeared as if they would overtake those on the bottom and get the chance to kill Indians.

When the last of the infantry had crossed the ridge, Hump and his warriors from the wood train appeared and came up over the ridge behind them. Crazy Horse led Harper and the

other decoy warriors across the bottom and through the creek a number of times. This signal brought the hidden warriors down from the tall grass and brush on both sides of the hills above Peno Creek and Fetterman was surrounded.

It was a day of great honor for Harper and all of the warriors of the Sioux and Cheyenne nations. The Bluecoats screamed and ran for cover in all directions. Fetterman tried to keep them in order, commanding them to fire their single-shot Springfields in alternating rounds so that the warriors would not charge in when they saw the rods in the air, signaling that reloading was occurring. But the Bluecoats were young and afraid and many of them became frozen with terror as arrows fell on them like hail in a storm. Many warriors gained honor by riding among the Bluecoats, striking them with war clubs and driving lances and arrows through muscle and bone. The two frontiersmen killed many warriors with their repeating rifles before they finally died, teaching the warriors that these new rifles were very deadly.

The valley was filled with a blue haze from rifle smoke and Harper could not see where Fetterman was among his soldiers. Most had already fallen and many of the wounded were crawling around, their blood freezing on their hands and the fronts and backs of their uniforms. Warriors moved everywhere, screaming and shooting arrows and rifles or dragging their own wounded and dead from the frozen ground. The last of the Bluecoats had been killed where they had taken cover among some rocks high on the hillside and there was a report that more soldiers were coming out from the fort.

With the day nearly gone and the cold of oncoming nightfall fast approaching, the warriors performed the final act of humiliation upon the Bluecoats. The bodies were stripped and the work of knives and war clubs would make their lives in the land beyond very difficult. They were cut open and their insides strewn about; their hands and arms

and feet and trigger fingers were cut off and left separate from their trunks, so that they could not run or use their arms in the next life. Their man parts were cut away and stuffed into their mouths and their brains were removed and placed upon rocks, so that they would not be able to think. Finally, their eyes were taken out and also placed upon rocks, so that they would not be able to see. None of them would now be whole as they passed from this earth.

Harper watched with a number of other warriors as the relief column of soldiers came down into the small valley. They were led by a commander named Ten Eyck, who with his men began to sort through the mutilated dead, their eyes filled with tears and their mouths lined with vomit. Nothing had been left alive, not even a dog found whining over a fallen soldier. Fallen horses lay everywhere, bristling with arrows. It was a day that would cause unending nightmares for the Little White Chief Carrington and it told him that the warriors of these lands were far stronger and more clever in warfare than he had ever suspected. For Harper it meant the beginning of his life again as a respected warrior.

For Harper the return of the warm moons to these lands came in stark contrast to the years he remembered as a child, roaming wild and free while the new colors invaded the rising slopes to the mountains. Now the children stayed close to the lodges and only played within sight of their mothers or an elder who was watching them. Never did they roam the banks of the streams and rivers for long distances or make a full day's journey of climbing a far wooded hill as he had when a boy. All was far different and the fear of an attack by Bluecoats was ever present.

Since the fight against Fetterman and his forces, which the Oglala called the Battle of the Hundred Slain, there had been no new attacks on the Bluecoats at Phil Kearny. Intense cold had set in and snow covered the blood of those who had died there. The women of the Indian peoples still sang songs

of mourning for their lost warriors while working with fingers still healing from the loss of joints cut off at the gravesites. It seemed their long lengths of hair were continually cut short in mourning, as the death of a loved one was a continual thing now. Snow Fawn had cut her hair to above shoulder length when the slain warriors were brought back from the small bottom and the hillsides above Peno Creek. When Harper had asked her about it, she had told him it was in memory of Elk-Dancing-at-Night. She said that he had been killed at Sand Creek by Bluecoats and that the memory of it would never leave her. Though Harper had tried to speak with her over the course of the cold moons, she had remained distant from him and had turned her back to him whenever he came near.

Now that the warm moons had brought the birds back to nest in the trees and game to the grasslands, Harper tried once again to talk with the woman who had borne his son.

"Your hair is growing out again and will soon be as beautiful as it ever was," he told her while she gathered wood. "I hope your sadness has passed for good now."

"I know you have been wanting to speak to me for a long time," she said, "and I know you think that you would like to maybe take me as your wife, but things can never be as you want them. Never."

"Why not? Much time has passed since all of our troubles. You have not married again and we have a son who needs a father."

"He is gaining a lot of knowledge from my brother, his uncle," Snow Fawn said. "He sees that you have gained great honors among our people and he is glad for it. But he is not the same as you and he does not long for the same things as you. He is worried that you will not understand him."

"Does he ask about me?"

"Often. And he wants to get to know you. But he is afraid."

"How can he be afraid of his own father?"

"I have told you that he does not wish for the honors that you do and he worries that you will think less of him for it. He is forming his own ideas about life and is afraid his views will anger you."

"I feel as if I am a total stranger to the only family I have. It is as if I must be alone in any world I am put in to live."

"It might have been better if you had gone back to the Bluecoats with your friend, the one who plays the medicine songs. Though you already have great honors as a warrior once again, perhaps your life cannot be complete here with the Bad Faces."

"You say words that tear at my heart. You once loved me very much. Will that love never return? Or has it returned and you are pushing it away?"

Snow Fawn began to tremble and drop sticks of wood from the pile she was carrying back to the village. She stopped and did not let Harper pick them up for her, but returned them from the ground to her hands by herself.

"I do not know how I feel about you," she told Harper. "I must take time to let my feelings speak to me from inside."

"How long will that be?"

"I cannot say. But do not push me."

"What about Fox Boy?"

"He wants to get to know you, and I see nothing wrong with that. He is happy that you made a bow and arrows for him. He wants to tell you that. But be gentle with him and be patient."

Harper watched her walk away and decided he would find Fox Boy. Perhaps if he gained the boy's love this would break down some of the barriers that now existed between himself and Snow Fawn. He could wait no longer to find out Fox Boy's feelings and found him sitting on a small rise at the edge of the village. Laid across his knees was a small piece of tanned buffalo hide stretched tightly across a looped willow stem. He was mixing paints in rock bowls in front of him.

"We have not been able to talk much," Harper began, "and I thought it would be good if we could be together for a time."

Fox Boy looked quickly at his father and back down to the paints he was mixing. "Do you wish to watch me?"

Harper nodded and sat down. "Do you like the bow I gave you?"

"I practiced some with it this morning," Fox Boy answered.

"A good warrior can hit a target with his eyes closed."

Fox Boy began to touch the paint to the skin with a pointed stick. Soon the form of a pinto horse appeared.

"But there is plenty of time to practice with your bow now that the warm moons are here," Harper added. "I did not know you were interested in drawing pictures. That is something that is usually done when you are older, after you have learned the skills of hunting and warfare."

Fox Boy continued to draw. "I have been doing this for some time. A few of the warriors have asked me to paint war robes for them. One of the medicine men said that I have been given a gift and that I should make use of it."

Harper watched while Fox Boy outlined a horseman thrusting a long lance toward a huge bear with a humped back. The bear had exceptionally long teeth and claws, and the lance head was very long and sharp.

"Your mother liked to paint at times," Harper said to Fox Boy. "Does she still paint?"

"A little. But her heart is sad and she worries about me. I tell her things will be good in time, but she still worries."

Harper changed the subject. "Did you see a bear like the one you are drawing up there?" he asked, pointing to the jagged outline of the Bighorn Mountains in the distance.

Fox Boy squinted along his father's finger. "I have heard many stories of those mountains, but I have never been high into them."

"You mean you have never been to Cloud Peak?"

Fox Boy shook his head. "We do not travel very far. Mother says it is not like it was in the old days." He held the finished drawing out toward Harper. "Would you like to have this?"

Harper took the skin from Fox Boy and studied the lines of fresh paint that depicted the ever present struggle for survival. He fought to keep his hands from trembling as he held the gift from his son. The life within this stretched piece of hide seemed to pulse through his fingers, like blood from the heart. The same feelings that had come to Harper that night when he had held Fox Boy at Fort Laramie again flooded over him.

"Thank you, Fox Boy. It is very nice."

"You like it?"

"Very much. I will hang it in an important place." He pointed once again to Cloud Peak. "Would you like to see that high country?"

Fox Boy nodded. "Yes, but wouldn't we be in danger?"

"We will take fast ponies."

Fox Boy smiled. "I will practice my riding skills."

"When the snows have melted up there, we will go high to where the sky comes down," Harper nodded. "It will be fun."

Fox Boy's eyes were warm as they rested on his father. "I am glad you came back," he said. "Maybe some day Mother will be glad also. Now she does not know what happiness is, except when she takes me in her arms and holds me. But she needs more than that. It is hard for me to know about these things, except for what I hear from others my age. My uncle is very good to me, but I have always wondered about you."

Harper was surprised to see Fox Boy react so warmly toward him so quickly. "Then you know that I still have feelings for your mother and that I have always missed you both since seeing you at Fort Laramie?"

"If that were not true," Fox Boy said, "then you would not have stayed here and let the old Bluecoat, who was your

friend, ride away alone that day when you came. Mother told me that it meant only that you preferred the Oglala way of life to that of the *Wasicun*. But I think she knows better."

"Maybe time will help her decide what she feels," Harper said.

Fox Boy was gazing out at the mountains. "Yes, maybe time will answer many things."

CHAPTER 10

Harper rode with Fox Boy high into the mountains, along wooded trails where squirrels and jays chattered; they led their ponies across rocky hillsides and watched bighorn sheep teach their newborn lambs to climb. The air pushed softly across the pine-clad slopes and over the fresh meadows where wildflowers, grass, and shrubs were woven together into a mantle of many bright colors. Near a high stretch of rock a wolverine stopped, hissed, and was lost in a crevice near the top. "Good medicine," Harper told Fox Boy, and he nodded.

Finally they left the steep slopes to pull onto a high plateau covered with grazing *Wapiti*. The bulls moved among the cows and calves with antlers covered with the soft velvet of summer growth. Those who had reached their prime carried racks that swept high over their heads and far back to nearly the full length of their bodies. Their heads were all raised as Harper and Fox Boy rode past them, filling the meadow with a rich tan and brown.

Far below, such sights were now seldom seen. The game was gone and the land was barren and worn from the continual use by *Wasicun* livestock. The warm moons had already made the ground hot where the grass was grazed to nothing and the early rains had washed the topsoil into the streams and rivers, making them run dark with sediment. This high country was a fresh new land where the game had come to seek refuge and where the wind carried no squeaks from rolling wagon wheels.

Coming over the top of the foothills that touched the lower slopes of the mountains, Harper pointed to the Bozeman

Trail, where wagon people were moving both toward and away from them. There was a continual flow, even though the deaths of Fetterman and his soldiers during the previous cold moons had been reported in newspapers all over the country. Nothing could stop these people from coming out here now. They were even finding new ways in which to come.

Near the trail that ran east from Fort Laramie, where Harper had traveled with the wagon people after being taken by Deals from the Oglala village, a set of iron tracks was being laid to bring more of the *Wasicun* people out here on the huge and noisy Iron Horse. The valley of the Platte was now nearly void of all game, so great was the train's thunder and black smoke. Harper remembered this giant machine well from riding it often while living among the *Wasicun* in the East. He knew then that it would some day find its way out to this country and bring vast numbers of people with it.

Now was the worst time for this to happen, for the Oglala and all the Indian peoples were poor in horses. Most had been eaten to survive the winter and to keep the strength from leaving their bodies entirely. Only since stripping Fort Reno of most of their cavalry mounts had the Bad Faces once again been able to provide their warriors with good, strong ponies. There was added pressure from the addition of many new Bluecoats to all the forts. Instead of teaching them a lesson, the death of Fetterman had served to anger the Bluecoat leaders and drive them to revenge. Now they wanted all the Indian peoples to give up this land to live on reservations. It was said there would be plenty of food and clothing for the people and there would be no more hunger.

"You must learn the song of the warrior," Harper told Fox Boy as they rode. "I know well the lies of the Bluecoats, for I was a victim of their crooked ways. It must be in your heart to be strong and to learn to fight the Bluecoats so that they can be driven from these lands forever."

They stopped to eat and Fox Boy showed his father that he was skilled in the building of fires. They warmed pieces of buffalo hump on a stick.

"Is it wise to fight the Bluecoats?" Fox Boy asked.

Harper stopped chewing. "That is a strange question from a boy who loves this land as much as you do."

"Is it true that the Bluecoats and the *Wasicun* are as many as the blades of grass? And is it true that all the Indian peoples together are not as many as the number of *Wasicun* that live in the place to the south called Denver?"

"They are very màny," Harper answered. "But they do not understand this land and they will destroy themselves trying to live on it."

"Maybe some day they will all perish," Fox Boy argued, "because they do not know the land and how to use it. Before that happens the Indian peoples will have been driven out."

"You sound defeated before you have even sung your war song."

Fox Boy cut another piece of meat from the stick, looked at his father, and began to speak English.

"I am nearly eleven years old, Father. I am able to think for myself now, even though there is much I do not understand about all that is happening."

Harper stared at his son again. This was proving to be an interesting day. He then switched to English himself.

"Where did you learn English? Not from your mother. She hates the language."

"When we lived among the southern Cheyenne there was a boy who had come from a settlement. He said his parents had died from sickness and that he had lost his directions. He was nursed to health and decided to stay among us. He was older than me and could see that my blood was mixed. He taught me English, though Mother tried to keep him away from me. He was a good friend."

"Where is he now."

"He died at Sand Creek. I told him to come with us and

run into the hills. But he stripped off his shirt and held up his hands and yelled. The Bluecoats didn't even look; they just shot him."

"He must have taught you a lot more than just the English language."

"He was smart. He told me not to be blind and to consider all things. He said there are many, many lands that we know nothing of."

Harper stood up and put the fire out and let the afternoon breeze whip through his long blond hair. He had a son who painted war robes for the council members and spoke two languages and wanted to see what was beyond the farthest rise. "Let us go on," he then told Fox Boy. He had switched back to Sioux. "We have a lot more to talk about before we go back down to the village."

They crossed over the plateau and on to where they could look out over the vast valley on the western side of the mountains. Now midafternoon, the sun was painting the columns of rising rock in flowing gold. They found a place to sit on a rounded cliff that hung over twisted canyons of pine and juniper. Far away was a new land that Harper had seen from this place before, but had never been to. It was said that somewhere in that far distance Crazy Horse had gained honors and his name in a fight against Shoshones. Now the valley floor looked blue and shimmered in the heat.

"Out there is a different land," Harper said to Fox Boy. "But it is not as good as our own."

"Have you lived there to know?"

"No."

"The Shoshone people would not agree with you. They would say that their land is better than ours. And the Crow people to the north believe their lands are still better yet. I believe all lands can be good to those who live there, if they will only learn the land and be good to it."

"The *Wasicun* are in all the lands," Harper said. "There is no place left to go."

Fox Boy looked out across the canyon where eagles had gathered and had spread themselves to the wind.

"I have never asked you about the blue coat you always wear," Fox Boy said. "Mother says it is a medicine coat."

"It was given to me by a special friend among the Blue-coats. It has become a part of my life."

"I hear you play the small flute that you carry in the coat."

"It, too, was a gift."

"You often play the medicine songs that the old Bluecoat played that day you came to the village to fight. You must like these songs."

"Yes. The old Bluecoat taught me those songs, and I taught him many Sioux songs."

Fox Boy was still watching the eagles glide in slow circles.

"What if you meet this special Bluecoat friend on the field of battle, Father?"

"He has gone north to where the *Wasicun* wagons go to find the shiny metal that makes them rich."

Fox Boy turned to him. "You know this?"

"He told me he wanted to go there as soon as possible. I believe he is there now. Why do you ask about my Bluecoat friend?"

Fox Boy had turned back to the eagles and was now watching a large dark one descend toward a slope of rocks and fallen timber below.

"I can tell that you still do not live in the world of the Oglala completely," Fox Boy answered, his eyes on the eagle. "The warriors in the village can see this also. I have heard Crazy Horse talk of it to others. I see Red Cloud staring at you. Whenever you play the medicine songs of the old Bluecoat, it reminds all in the village of battle. It reminds them of death and lost loved ones. It reminds Mother of her dead husband."

"I did not know this."

"You cannot see it, for the *Wasicun* songs mean as much to you as the Sioux songs. And I know if some day you meet the

old Bluecoat in battle, you will not be able to kill him. Then the warriors in the village will wonder what is truly in your heart. They might drive you away, or even kill you."

The eagle that Fox Boy had been watching had now plummeted, wings folded, into the rocks and timber of the slope below, looking as if it had crashed. It rose momentarily with a kicking, fat marmot in its talons.

Harper watched the eagle rise to a nest among the rocks high along the cliffs and turned to his son.

"Why did you not tell me what you were thinking before this?"

"How could I have told you?" Fox Boy said. "You would have thought that I shared the same conflict of feelings inside that my mother has for you, and that I was saying things to try and drive you away so that she might have peace within herself."

"Does she hate me, Fox Boy?"

"She hates what you did to her, but she cannot bring herself to hate you. There are times when her eyes show that she is thinking about the past, when she loved you and hoped to go into a lodge with you as your wife. But she always makes her face go hard and drives those memories out."

Another eagle had dropped into the tangle of rocks below to come up with another marmot. It reminded Harper of the times he had watched the eagles fish the rivers when the seasons changed, and how they all had found the one place where the fish were swimming up though rocks slick and shiny in the rapids. It seemed life was easy for them, just flying to where the food was and hatching eggs once a year.

"I want to make those memories good once again," Harper told Fox Boy. "Do you think your mother could ever think of me as she once did?"

Fox Boy shrugged and began to pick at some dried paint on his fingers. "I cannot say."

"Is she glad that you want to come with me at times?"

"Yes. But she does not want to influence me by what she feels. She tells me that you are my father and that I am of your blood, and that I should always care about you."

Harper nodded. He watched Fox Boy continue to work on the dried paint clinging to his fingers. "Things will again be good," he finally said. "They will be good in time. Now there is much pressure from the Bluecoats and all of us are under great strain. It affects our thinking. When the Bluecoats are driven out, things will again be good and your mother will have time to think about us becoming a family."

Fox Boy looked up at his father. "We will not drive the Bluecoats out," he said matter-of-factly. "Why do you refuse to accept something that is very plain?"

"We *have* to drive them out. There is no choice."

"Why is it so bad to think of going someplace where there are no *Wasicun,* someplace they do not wish to be?"

"Soon they will be everywhere and they will want to own everything. There is no place to go. Do you understand that? Can you accept what I am telling you?"

"Yes, but I do not agree that fighting them as we have been is ever going to bring us victory. We kill a few of them here and there, and they are then replaced by ten times as many. Our warriors spend valuable time fighting this way when they should be hunting. It is my feeling that *all* the Indian peoples should gather in council and make a plan to resist the *Wasicun* movement into these lands. *All* the tribes of *all* these lands should come together. The past hatreds and wars would have to be forgotten. There is no other way. And if this cannot be done then we must stop the fighting and keep the *Wasicun* from building up any more hate against us."

"There would be no honor in giving up," Harper said.

"What is honorable about this fighting?" Fox Boy asked. "The elders speak often of the days when Indian peoples fought one another and it was a matter of honor. They would face one another and tell one another that there was going to be a fight between them. The winner gained honor.

The Bluecoats do not kill us for honor, except for their leaders, who have confused honor with the accumulation of dead bodies. They wish only to get rid of us and will do it in any manner they can."

"It is not possible to think of getting the Indian peoples all together," Harper told Fox Boy. "There is too much hatred, and already many of our enemies have sided with the Bluecoats and act as scouts for them. Now even more hatred has resulted."

"Maybe this can be changed," Fox Boy said. "If someone told them that they were fighting against their own people and that they could return to their old ways if they stopped this and joined together, maybe they would listen."

Harper thought for a time. Fox Boy seemed to have wisdom beyond his years. What he had been saying was all perfectly true, and it was certain that the Sioux and Cheyenne peoples could never stop the flow of Bluecoats. Even with the Arapaho as an ally, there was no chance. But the thought of bringing together old enemies from countless winters of warfare seemed even more remote than victory for the northern plains tribes without help from others. Fox Boy could see the plight and the hopeless situation facing a people he was just coming of age among. To Harper it seemed as though his son might be gifted by other than a talent for drawing and painting. Perhaps he was a dreamer, one of those selected by the spirits to witness events within their mind before they happened. Such a gift was treated with the utmost respect and honor. Such a gift was a mark of great distinction.

"Has your mind ever given you visions of things to come?" Harper asked Fox Boy.

Fox Boy looked startled, as if his father had made a discovery that he was not yet ready to reveal.

"It is nothing to be afraid of," Harper told his son. "You probably cannot understand it and you might even be afraid of it, but this is a good gift to have."

"Things have come to me," Fox Boy admitted, "especially during the cold moons when there has been little to eat and I have become weakened. It seems there were times when my mind traveled from my body and went to places I know nothing of. Many times I was frightened."

"Have you spoken with your mother about this?"

"She would only worry about me, and never let me out of her sight. Some of the things I have seen are terrible. I never want her to know about one of them, for I know I saw the fighting at Sand Creek in a dream a full winter before it happened."

Harper moved closer to his son. "Do you wish to tell me what you saw?"

Fox Boy's face was tight with pain.

"It would be good if you could tell me," Harper coaxed.

"It came in the form of an antelope kill," Fox Boy began, "much the same as when hunting warriors drive a herd into a river and up against a steep bank, where they crush their skulls with clubs. In my dream the river had ice all along the banks and the Cheyenne people were antelope with human faces. They were running and screaming into the river while Bluecoats crashed through the ice and into the water behind them. At the edge of the river, near the high bank, a tall lodgepole had been driven deep into the bed below the water and a flag that was striped with red and white, and had blue on it with stars, was placed at the top. Black Kettle had swum to this flag and all the Cheyenne people, with their faces crying on their antelope bodies, gathered around the flag. Black Kettle was yelling, 'We are your friends! We are your friends!' and the very old warrior, White Antelope, was yelling, 'Stop! Please stop!'

"But the Bluecoats paid no attention and they rushed among the Cheyenne antelope-people and drove them away from the flag and back up against the high cliff where they could not get away. The antelope-people thrashed and screamed and sank in the current while the Bluecoats

clubbed them and shot them and drove their sabres into them. And I saw my mother's face on an antelope, trying to drag Elk-Dancing-at-Night away from the flag. But he was having one of his blind and confused spells, and he tore away from her. Then a Bluecoat shot him in the face and my mother cried as she swam underwater to get away from the killing."

Harper was holding Fox Boy while he sobbed uncontrollably. His tears soaked the front of Harper's blue medicine coat and he shook spasmodically as all of the terror rose again in his mind. After a time Fox Boy stopped crying, but continued to keep his arms around his father.

"Nothing like that will ever happen again," Harper told him.

"But it will," Fox Boy said quickly. "I could not stand to have another dream of that kind."

"You spoke of Elk-Dancing-at-Night. What did you mean about his being blind and confused?"

"When I was very young, he came back from a raid against *Wasicun* wagon people with bad injuries to his head. I do not remember it and Mother will not speak about it. I learned that he had been struck in the face with a rifle and that this hurt his head so that he could not remember well after that. There were times when his vision would fail also, and he would wander about in a daze. Mother loved him and was always sad about this, but there was nothing any of the medicine men could do. He could never go on war parties again and he fell off his pony often while hunting, but he would never talk about any of it to me."

Harper's mind went back to the day of the fight with the warriors who had come with Red Cloud. Elk-Dancing had wished to gain great honors that day and Harper had stopped him with the Springfield. As Fox Boy had just described it, he had also ended Elk-Dancing's life in the normal world. There was no other way it could have been and Harper knew if he had it to do over again, he would

have to fight as well as he had that day. Had Elk-Dancing counted coup against him, his life would surely have been taken from him. O'Leary and the wagon people would have also died and Elk-Dancing and the warriors with Red Cloud would have returned to their villages with honors.

Harper knew he could not explain this to Fox Boy now. Maybe it was better for a time that Fox Boy not know that it was his father who had struck Elk-Dancing with the rifle that day eight winters past. For Harper the memory of that day had now changed: he was sorry that he had taken the lives of the two warriors and had injured Elk-Dancing so badly. His choice could not have been otherwise, for O'Leary would have been killed along with Dawson had he not acted when he did. But the fact that the *Wasicun* wagon people had then turned on him in hatred and had blamed him for the deaths of Dawson and the small girl now burned even deeper into him. Men like O'Leary were rare among the *Wasicun* people; most all the rest were content to follow the lead of others without question, like small calves follow the herds, and despised those who did not follow in line with them. Harper swore with even more determination that he would never fall in line for any reason, even if the Oglala were forced to do so. He would always remain free to make his own choices. He could only hope now that he would have a wife and son who would follow him.

CHAPTER 11

The warm moons were passing quickly and the time for the Sun Dance had come. Harper was grateful to the spirits and to *Wakan' Tanka* for bringing him to Fox Boy and for allowing a closeness to grow between them. He took part in the Sun Dance once again, and during the Holy Days of the ceremony he was painted and dressed in the sacred way. He danced and bled with the others from new wounds in his chest that soon closed and began to heal beneath the scars of many winters past.

Harper no longer played the penny whistle that O'Leary had given him. Instead, he placed it inside a special skin pouch he made for it and put it away. He did not want to remind any of his people of lost relatives and loved ones, and he did not want to give Snow Fawn any reason to think worse of him.

Now that he and Fox Boy were spending a lot of time together, Harper thought he could detect a slight change in Snow Fawn. Perhaps she would now be more receptive to him. She talked to him longer each time they spoke and seemed pleased that Fox Boy had grown much happier. Still there was a certain barrier that she kept between Harper and herself and Harper decided that now was the time to try and once again win her love.

Harper was certain that he could bring Snow Fawn's love to him in the traditional way, as he had before when they were both young. He would need to make a love flute, with the head of the special bird, a redheaded woodpecker, carved into its end. He had done this those many winters past and the legend of the first flute came back to him as he

prepared himself to find the wood for the flute. It was a story handed down for longer than anyone could remember. It was spoken of as the legend of *Siyotanka* and told how a young man found the first love flute while hunting for elk. The young man had followed a herd into a deep forest along a river, staying just out of bow range from him. It became late and he was forced to make his bed in the darkness of the forest, while owls and wolves gave their calls and branches creaked in the wind.

All throughout this dark night the young man was kept from sleep by a strange, haunting sound that rose over the calls of the wild animals. He was at first frightened by this call but then became fascinated by its rich musical quality, which spoke to him of love. When the morning came, the young man watched a redheaded woodpecker hammer against a tree with its sharp bill. The bird seemed to beckon the young hunter and he followed the woodpecker to a hollow tree where a dead limb had been filled with holes from the woodpecker's beak. The wind cried through this dead limb, making the strange call of love the young man had heard through the night. The young man then climbed the dead tree and cut the limb off. He spent the day trying to play the songs he had heard and realized that the best wood to use was that of the cedar. The elk never left him and watched, teaching him the songs of love that came from the flute. The young man then forgot the hunt and returned to his village to play the songs he had learned from the elk, quickly winning the love of a young woman.

So now it was always said that if anyone had the elk medicine and knew the songs on the flute of the redheaded woodpecker, he could win the love of anyone he desired.

Harper went into the hills where the cedar grew thick on the slopes and found a round branch of good size. He cut and trimmed it, and worked a hole down through its length with a bowstring drill. Throughout the entire day he cut and whittled and polished, praying to the spirits that his hand

might again perform the magic that had once brought Snow Fawn to him. When the design of the love flute was finished, he held it in the smoke of sacred sage and cedar leaves. The end had been carved in the shape of a woodpecker's head and he now painted it red. The neck was painted a glossy black. When he had finished, he started back for the village and sang those songs that would make his elk medicine good and bring the lyrics of love to the flute when he played it.

It was late in the night when he reached the village and he decided to take a place in the trees and brush near the river where the women always went for water each morning. He found it hard to sleep and heard owls and wolves nearby, but there came no sound of wind singing through a dead limb. His hope for the legend of *Siyotanka* to come to him in this place would not happen. Still, he had the love flute and knew its medicine was strong.

When the sun finally rose, the women walked along the trail to the river in small groups, talking and laughing as they filled their skin bags with water. Finally Snow Fawn appeared with two others and Harper began his song from back among the trees.

The other two women pointed and looked back from their work as Harper played, but Snow Fawn paid no attention. She talked with the others and filled her skin bags without bothering to look over her shoulder once. Finally Harper stopped his playing and walked out from the trees. The women with Snow Fawn hurried quickly away.

"Did you not hear my song?" Harper asked Snow Fawn.

"I heard you, but I did not care to listen."

"You did not like my song?"

"The song is beautiful. But you are wasting your time playing it for me."

Harper frowned. "I had thought that maybe time would change your mind."

Snow Fawn was squeezing one of the skin bags she had filled with water and turning it over in her hands. "I do not

hold the past against you, but I see nothing for us together in the future. I asked you to give me time to let my inner feelings speak to me and you have given me this time. Now I must tell you what those feelings are, and they are nothing."

"When we were young, your feelings were very strong. Can it never be that way between us again?"

"When a woman is young her heart beats faster and her dreams are bigger. When she grows older she must some day face herself and realize that life is not meant to be a dream. My dream was broken when you did not take me for your wife. Ever since that day I knew my life would not be as I had imagined it."

"I have suffered as much as you over the past," Harper said. "Perhaps more. But now is another time and there is no reason why we must live with other things eating the inside of us."

"I have been thinking about the past," Snow Fawn said quickly, "and I am not sure that it was you or your music I fell in love with."

"You are just trying to hurt me."

"I am trying to tell you that I am not sure even now how I felt then. Young people fall in love easier than those who have seen more years."

Harper could not keep his eyes off Snow Fawn. Her hair had grown out again and was glossy and full, her face as clean and pure as the mountain waters that came down to this river. He wanted to reach out and pull her to him, to once again feel the warmth and tenderness that she had given him so many winters past. He wanted to feel her snuggle close to him again and put her arms around his neck, and then pull his lips down to hers. It could not happen, he knew, and to try and make it happen by drawing her to him would surely drive her away.

"We were in love then," Harper told her. "Both of us. You were in love and so was I. My mistake was in not listening to my heart."

"I do not think your heart spoke to you then," Snow Fawn said. "That is why I did not tell you about Fox Boy."

"I wish you had."

"I wanted you to take me for what I was, not for the child we made between us."

Harper shuffled his feet. "Fox Boy is glad I came back. I believe he wishes we could get back together."

"It is good that Fox Boy has wanted to give his love to you. This is only right, for you are his father and he knows that you love him very much. But I do not intend to do anything that would hurt him. I am afraid that if I was to become your wife, it would eventually make us both unhappy. And Fox Boy would then suffer also. I do not want this and I am sure you do not either."

Harper nodded. "I will respect your wishes. It will be as you wish it, and I will not play the love flute for you again. But I will always wish my songs could have reached you as they once did."

Snow Fawn turned quickly away and hurried back toward the village with her water skins. She dropped one and stooped to pick it up, keeping her back to Harper as she grabbed at it to keep from spilling any more water. Harper turned to face the river and considered throwing the love flute into the current. But he stopped himself and turned back toward the village, where he placed it in the skin bag with the penny whistle.

The warm moons were ending and the early frost of the season when the leaves change had crept into the night. The first signs of yellow had worked through the cottonwoods along the river and when the breezes touched their leaves, shimmers of sunlight came from them. High in the foothills and mountains, the cottonwood's cousin, the aspen, was already covered with the golden robes of its late season glory as it waited for the snows to make the land white.

The Indian peoples of these lands had all seen much

fighting and now the Bluecoats were shouting victory nearly each time. There had been a fight in a hayfield near Fort C.F. Smith where many Cheyenne had been killed while few Bluecoats and *Wasicun* haycutters had been injured or killed. Harper had gone with Red Cloud and Crazy Horse to Phil Kearny, where a great many warriors were killed the next day while attacking a wood train. War for the Indian peoples had now turned very bad, for the Bluecoats and the *Wasicun* people traveling the Bozeman Trail all had repeating rifles.

So very suddenly the fighting power of the Bluecoat soldiers had changed to one of superior strength. With these new rifles, they could fire very fast and each single soldier now had the strength of seven who had once carried the Springfield muzzle-loaders. Harper thought very often now about what Fox Boy had said that day in the Bighorn Mountains when they had watched the eagles. If the Indian peoples had all joined together in the very beginning, they could have swept down the Bozeman Trail and burned every fort along it, including the powerful Fort Laramie. Now it was too late and the death of Fetterman and his men had told the Bluecoat chiefs that the Indian peoples could fight and that a great deal of power would be needed to stop them. That power had finally come.

Fox Boy stood on the back of his pony, carving pictures high on the face of a large sandstone rock. Harper watched for a time while Fox Boy chipped away with a sharpened piece of steel rod that had been taken from a burned wagon. Many ponies were taking shape on the face of the rock and it appeared as if they were all running.

"We are going to fight now," Harper told Fox Boy. "It would be good if you went back to the village now."

"I must finish this first," Fox Boy said. "Then I will go back."

"I worry about your safety. And I told your mother that I would be able to talk you into returning to the village."

"I will be done before long. Then I will go back and tell her

that you spoke with me and that I would not listen. She will understand."

Harper rode away to join the other warriors who were waiting for him. There was something in Fox Boy's eyes now that worried him. It seemed as if the boy had been drawn to the rock to complete the drawing and that his compulsion overshadowed even the threat of danger.

"Do you still wish to lead this war party?" one of the warriors asked. "You act as if you have seen a bad omen."

"No," Harper answered quickly. "We will fight."

The war party was small and had been organized quickly in response to the word from a village scout who announced he had seen a number of Bluecoat and *Wasicun* riders going through the hills at the foot of the mountains. Harper had spoken up that he would lead warriors against them, whoever they might be, and bring back new repeating rifles for all the warriors. Red Cloud and Crazy Horse had already begun to make plans for a large attack against a long train of the white-topped wagons that were said to be coming north into these lands. It was said that this long train of wagons was under escort by a great number of Bluecoats, led by a white chief dressed in dark buckskins and wearing a strange sort of hat.

This was to be the main fight and a great many warriors were already making preparations to follow Red Cloud and Crazy Horse. Then, hearing about getting the new rifles, nearly fifty warriors joined Harper to go after the smaller party of Bluecoats and *Wasicun* riders. There was something unusual, Harper told them, about a group of Bluecoats and *Wasicun* who traveled alone on horseback and off the main trail.

They found this group of Bluecoats and *Wasicun,* just one short of twenty in number, riding through the draws of the foothills just below the mountains. It was plain that they had hoped to sneak past the Indian villages and out of the area before being detected. This was not to be and Harper

screamed a war cry as he led the warriors down through the hills.

It was a running fight from the beginning, the Bluecoats and *Wasicun* riders scattering like prairie hens before wolves. They went in all directions, up different draws and across many small creeks. They were not organized and many of them appeared to be very young. The warriors ran a good many of them down, shooting them from their saddles at point-blank range with arrows and rifles. Those who had fallen and were not dead returned fire from the ground with their repeating rifles. Warriors fell also.

One small group that had stayed together left their horses and took cover in some rocks at the top of a hill. Harper heard warriors yelling for help in killing them and he sent everyone over, for it now appeared that all the other Bluecoats and *Wasicun* had been found and killed.

Harper was turning his pony to join the others when he noticed two riders going up a small draw off a ways from where the fighting was taking place. Quickly he followed them and fitted an arrow to his bow. One of them turned his horse and began shooting with a repeating rifle. The bullets whizzed past Harper and, as he released an arrow, he felt a searing pain drive its way through his left side.

The rider dropped the repeating rifle and fell from his horse, Harper's arrow having driven itself through his abdomen and out through his back. Harper watched the other rider, a Bluecoat, spur his horse wildly for the top of the little draw. He would cross over in a matter of moments.

Harper got down from his pony, blood trailing from the wound in his side down across his left leg. He picked up the repeating rifle and fired quickly at the Bluecoat rider now nearing the top of the draw. The horse under the Bluecoat squealed and fell, rolling sideways onto the Bluecoat's leg. The horse kicked a few times before it died, pushing itself further onto the Bluecoat, who yelled from underneath.

The other fallen rider was lying doubled up on the

ground, the arrow through his lower back moving jerkily with his spasmodic breathing. His eyes were dazed and he was trying to speak to someone who was not there. Harper put the muzzle of the rifle against his temple and pulled the trigger before taking a cartridge belt from around his middle.

After reloading the rifle, Harper walked up the hill to where the Bluecoat was working his way out from under the fallen horse. His hair was almost completely white and Harper noticed lines of red mixed with it.

"Hell of a way to meet up again, ain't it, lad?" O'Leary was out of breath and grimmacing from pain in his leg trapped under the horse. "I wish you hadn't shot me horse, lad."

"I didn't know it was you," Harper stuttered. "You've lost a whole lot of weight, and your hair is nearly snow white."

Harper helped O'Leary out from under the horse and felt his leg.

"Strained a bit maybe," he told O'Leary, "but nothing broken. Where have you been? I thought you were going out of this land a long time ago."

"Things ain't gone well for me, lad," O'Leary said. "I got down to Fort Reno after leaving you with your boy and who should show up there but Cornhead Deals. He had me thrown in the guardhouse and was set to court-martial me. He wanted to see me hang bad, me boy, but his orders for court-martial were slow and he had to go back down to Laramie. He made the fort commander keep me in the guard house all winter. They don't feed you well, lad, and I ain't fully recovered yet."

"How did you get way up here?" Harper asked.

"A bunch of teamsters lost their wagons to Injuns just below Reno a ways. They came to the fort and were told to wait until the next bunch of wagons came through. Some of them got into a fight with a bunch of soldiers and ended up in the guardhouse with me. I figured their friends would break them out and talked them into takin' me along. We

broke free of Reno about midnight and shot a bunch of soldiers doin' it. We just about made it clean outta this country, too. Damned if you ain't the fighter, no matter which side you're on."

Harper was looking back over the hills. The fighting in the draw a ways away had slowed and it was certain some of the warriors would find this place soon.

"You gave me a pony once when it should have been yours," Harper said to O'Leary. "Take mine and leave now, before the others find us."

Harper helped O'Leary atop his pony and watched him climb the draw and disappear over the top. O'Leary was worried about the wound in Harper's side but finally laughed and agreed that his blood was too thick to run out of a little hole that size. O'Leary had called him a friend for life just before he left and said that, white or Indian, Harper had done more for him than any man since his father.

Harper was walking down the draw past the dead rider with the arrow through his abdomen when a group of warriors rode across from a far hill and waved scalps and repeating rifles. They saw the wound in Harper's side and nodded their approval. He could now paint a ring around his wound to show he had received it in battle against an enemy. Harper felt his back where the bullet was lodged between the skin and his ribs. He wished it had gone all the way through. He lay on his back while a warrior heated a knife over a fire and worked the bullet out through a cut he made in Harper's back. Then the wound was cauterized with the hot blade and Harper took a horse that had belonged to a fallen Bluecoat and rode it back to the village.

CHAPTER 12

The war drums were sounding and the village was alive with dancing as every warrior able to fight was preparing to follow Red Cloud and Crazy Horse when the sun came again. Harper ignored the fire and deep ache in his side as he searched the outer circle for Fox Boy and Snow Fawn. He moved among everyone, accepting congratulations for the war party's success, but saw no sign of them. Then a touch against his arm turned him to face Snow Fawn.

"He is gone," she said of Fox Boy, her eyes filled with worry in the light of the fires. "He returned from where he had been carving on the sandstone and said that he must leave again. I did not want him to go because of the Blue-coats that are so near, but he told me he had to search out his dream."

"Did he tell you about his dream?"

"He never tells me about his dreams. He knows I will worry." She noticed Harper's side. "You have been shot."

"I am not hurt badly and there is no more bleeding. Did Fox Boy say anything about what he must do?"

"I heard him say something about eagles and how they fell from the sky, and that he must go there and speak to the wind."

Harper turned from the circle of light and began to walk toward the horse herd. Snow Fawn ran behind him.

"Where are you going?" she asked. "Do you know where he is?"

"In the mountains," Harper answered. "There is a place of eagles high among the rocks. I must go there now, for it is a long journey."

Harper caught one of his ponies, one that was strong and good at climbing, and prepared for his journey into the mountains to find Fox Boy. He packed food and made sure all his weapons were ready for use and then took his pony to the river for water. While the horse drank he allowed Snow Fawn to place a poultice of dried herbs against the wounds on his lower side and back and tie them into place with a long strip of cloth around his middle.

"Riding so far and so hard will not be good for your wound," she said. "This will help it to heal properly."

When she was finished Harper took her in his arms and she did not resist. He kissed her softly and let the rising moon shine into her eyes.

"You know my feelings for you," he told her. "And you know I will do anything to make up for how I once hurt you. I want you and Fox Boy with me always."

"I believe you," she said. "Maybe my hurt will never completely go away but I realized that day when I talked with you at the river how much I had been resisting the voice within me. It had not told me to tell you to stop playing for me; it had told me to forget the past and to make myself happy once again, while I still can. Fox Boy has left and now you come back from a raid with a bullet hole in your side. I could lose everything so very quickly."

Harper kissed her again and they held each other for a time. It was so very good to feel her close once more. She would regain her happiness and, in time, perhaps let the past fall away completely.

"I want you to come back with our son," she told him. "Soon."

Harper ran his fingers through her long hair and held it out for the moonlight to touch. She was blinking back tears. She was so very beautiful.

"Go," she whispered.

"I will come back with our son. Soon."

Harper climbed on his pony and Snow Fawn disappeared

along the trail back to the village. He let the pony swim the current of the river slowly while he studied the night around him. The moon was changing, nearly full, and the blanket of white light made the mountains loom big against the dense blackness behind. Light frost crept through the air and the sound of geese flying south carried down from high above. They crossed in front of the huge pale moon, flying in a V that was long and uneven.

He rode toward the huge jagged mass that was the Bighorns, the night making them seem within his reach. He switched the heavy repeating rifle from arm to arm as he rode, his pony settling into a slow but steady gallop that ate up the rolling hills and streams and long grassy benches that formed the valley. He forgot about the wound in his side and did not notice the jolting and bouncing that brought trickles of blood and clear liquid from the holes in him. His knees gripped the pony's ribs for balance as his mind traveled out through the night to where he imagined Fox Boy to be. He kicked the pony into a faster gallop, wishing he had already reached the cliff where the eagles circled.

Harper found Fox Boy sitting cross-legged on the large rock where they had watched the eagles soar across the valley to the west. The sun was just climbing the eastern horizon and the sky was clear and blue. Harper jumped from the pony and Fox Boy ran to embrace him.

"Father, I knew you would come."

"I and your mother have been very worried about you. She told me you spoke of a dream."

"While I was drawing on the sandstone, the faces of many soldiers appeared to me. The white chief who wears dark buckskins, who ran with the Bluecoats the day you came to live with us, was leading them. They came to destroy our village, as the white chief Chivington did at Sand Creek."

Harper looked for fear in Fox Boy's eyes, but saw none. Instead there was confidence.

"This dream did not scare you as the one about Sand Creek?" Harper asked him.

Fox Boy was smiling. "The Bluecoats turned and ran in the wind and rain. They whipped their ponies and cried out in fear, for they saw me and you, Father. They saw us and were afraid."

"I do not understand."

Fox Boy appeared to be in a trance. "We must hurry down off the mountain to the river. We must reach the Bluecoats this day." Fox Boy was on his pony and had kicked it into a run across the plateau before Harper could call out to him.

When Harper caught up to Fox Boy he learned that they were both to play a major part in stopping Deals from reaching the village with his soldiers. Harper told Fox Boy that Deals and the Bluecoats who followed him were escorting a wagon train along the Bozeman Trail and that Red Cloud and Crazy Horse were now leading warriors to intercept and attack it. Fox Boy shook his head and said that in his dream he had seen only Bluecoat soldiers, a river, and wagons the Bluecoats used to carry their dead and wounded. This and his father with a many-shoots rifle, and himself as a spirit creature.

Harper looked at his repeating rifle and realized that Fox Boy could not have even known he would have this rifle when his dream occurred. At the sandstone rock, Harper had had only a bow and arrows. The spirits were indeed speaking with his son and it was an eerie feeling.

The day became very warm and the sun had passed midday when they reached the foothills below the mountains. A wind was stirring the tops of the pines and junipers, pushing dust clouds up from the Bozeman Trail where the wagons and livestock had churned the dry autumn ground to powder. Through his spy glass, Harper could see the long column of white-topped wagons coming through the hills near the crossing at Crazy Woman Fork. They moved slowly and awkwardly, and it left a bitter taste in his mouth.

To the east rose the dust cloud formed by the warriors of Red Cloud and Crazy Horse as they came to intercept the wagons before they reached the big waters the Bluecoats called Lake DeSmet. Here, between forts Reno and Phil Kearny, they could attack knowing the Bluecoats would have a good distance to travel to save the wagon people.

Harper knew that Deals and his command had left their wagons near Fort Reno and were marching along Powder River toward the village. They would never be seen by the war party. How Fox Boy had seen all this in a dream seemed beyond imagination.

As they neared Powder River, still a ways above the village, Harper could see through his spy glass that Deals and his marching Bluecoats were coming through the bottom. A distance ahead of them were three Pawnee scouts who watched the hills around them and spoke about fighting their old enemies. A cloud had passed over the mountains and the heat in the valley was making it black and rolling as it came. Soon its belly was spitting streaks of lightning that burned the hot afternoon ground.

"The wind has come as promised," Fox Boy said. "The time to get ready is here."

Harper followed Fox Boy down into the cover of trees and brush along the river. Lightning continued to flash from the oncoming bank of dark clouds and deep rumbling roars echoed through the skies. It made the afternoon suddenly dark, except for the light that came down in unusual streaks through the tattered edge of the storm.

Fox Boy had begun a medicine song sacred to his dream and he took from a small skin bag a number of materials to mix for paint. Using river water, he mixed various colors as he sang and spread them over his body. He dyed his head and body a dark red and worked clay into his hair to make it stick out in all directions, like stiff, pointed projections. He painted streaks of jagged lightning down his arms and chest and legs. Finally he drew large blue circles around his eyes,

wrists, and ankles. He was stripped to only a breechclout and he appeared hideous.

The dark cloud moved overhead and strange scattered winds began to move the tops of isolated trees and spread dust over sections of the valley, while other places remained calm and without disturbance. The Pawnee scouts watched the sky and began to sing songs to their spirits as they moved ever closer to where Harper waited with Fox Boy along the river.

The wind worked in mysterious ways as it sang loudly in groves of trees and along hillsides. A whirling dust devil started its crazy circle of zig-zag motion at the base of a nearby hill and pushed quickly across the bottom until it finally turned and became lost in the cottonwoods not far from Harper and Fox Boy.

"The winds spirit has come," Fox Boy said, his eyes wide. "My time is now."

The Pawnee scouts had stopped their ponies at the first sight of the dust devil and now thought it had gone into the trees to hide. Fox Boy rushed out onto the bottom not far from them, making it appear as if the dust devil had now taken the form of a wind spirit. He began to scream and dance toward them, making sign that he had come from the black cloud overhead to kill them and to spread the Blue-coats for the wolves. He mixed his sign with screeches and an Oglala war song that echoed as far back as Deals and his command, who had stopped to watch the Pawnee scouts.

A wind spirit who sang war songs. To the Pawnee scouts it was a very bad omen. They turned their ponies and frantically whipped them into a dead run back up the valley and past Deals, who was yelling for them to come back. The scouts would not stop their ponies until they had got out from under the huge cloud that spit lightning and wind spirits. Their yelling carried far out as they rode and the confused Bluecoats now were looking at the hills just behind them.

A dead pine, crackling in flames from a bolt of lightning, was throwing sparks out into the dry grass. A blaze quickly broke out and grew like a wall toward the soldiers, pinning them against the river. They broke formation and scattered like birds in flight.

To escape the billowing flames, they plunged into the river and swam frantically toward the opposite shore. The wind whipped the fire up through the hills and out onto the rising benches and plateaus above the river, making the black sky overhead even blacker. Some of the soldiers became hung up in the trees and brush while they frantically clawed their way toward the water and the flames caught them and made them whirling, twisting balls of fire. Horses squealed in terror and bucked and thrashed in the water, while some of the Bluecoats tried to go back and help those trapped by fallen trees. Soon the smoke had choked and blinded many so that they ran in the wrong direction and right into the fire.

Deals had his pistol drawn and was aiming it at a group of soldiers he had ordered to find the field cannons. They were shaking their heads and one of them fell as his pistol coughed smoke. Two others had now come forward and were aiming their rifles at Deals, who turned his horse and spurred it back down the valley as bullets whined around him. The horse fell and he rose to his feet, seeing soldiers running toward him from back near the fire.

He began to run, turning his head to see if they were gaining on him. He had spurred his horse a good distance before it had fallen from the rifle fire. If he could make it around this bend in the river, he would be able to find cover and hide from them.

Harper leveled the repeating rifle and Deals heard it click as a cartridge was levered into the barrel.

"Harper! No!"

His eyes were wide and wild as three successive shots entered his chest cavity. Driven backwards, Deals turned and stumbled, holding his chest, and fell across the English safari

hat that slipped from his head. Harper and Fox Boy jumped onto their ponies and became lost in the cover of the smoke as the other Bluecoats ran up to Deals and looked around in wonderment at who had shot him. It then occurred to them that there might well be Indians nearby and they all turned and ran. Then one of them came back, looking around him in jerky motions, and blew a hole in Deals's forehead with his pistol.

Harper and Fox Boy moved out across the hills toward the waters called DeSmet to find Red Cloud and the warriors with him. Smoke rolled out of the bottom and from the large wall of flame that was moving toward the village. Though the horses had grazed most of the grass near the village, there were a number of trees that could carry the fire to the village.

"We do not need to worry," Fox Boy said. "The wind spirits have spoken harshly to the Bluecoats and now there will be rain to cool the land." Fox Boy pointed toward the mountains where a parting in the veil of smoke revealed streaks of distant rain. The storm began as light intermittent drops but by the time they came in sight of Red Cloud and the warriors near Lake DeSmet, it had turned into a steady rain.

"You bring a spirit with you to fight against the Bluecoats with us," Red Cloud told Harper as warriors parted widely to let him and Fox Boy through.

"It is Fox Boy who was a spirit this day," Harper said. He pointed to where the rain was blanketing the fire back along the river. "The Bluecoats were going to the village and Fox Boy saw this in a dream."

The warriors began to talk among themselves. They had thought that the Bluecoats were afraid and would not come with the wagons. Now they were aware that their families had been in danger with only a few younger warriors and some elders to defend their camp.

"Fox Boy frightened the Pawnee scouts away and the thunder spirits set fire to the trees and grass around the Bluecoats, burning many of them up."

Now there was a lot of talk among the warriors. It was a

great honor to have had a dream; but to have lived one also was worthy of great acclaim. They gathered around Fox Boy and began to touch him so that they might receive some of his medicine.

"Father killed the white chief who wears the funny hat," Fox Boy said. "His dark buckskins were covered with blood, but his hair was not worthy of keeping. That man was of no honor whatsoever."

"It is a medicine day," Harper said.

Red Cloud agreed and pointed to where the wagons were coming down the slope onto the flat in the rain.

"Now it will be easy to kill all of the *Wasicun* people and burn their wagons."

The warriors all yelled their approval as they watched the wagons draw nearer. They would fight here and then go and try to catch the Bluecoats who were on their way back to Fort Reno. It would be a great day for the Sioux nation and it would cripple the Bluecoats.

The rain continued to fall and the wagons drew ever closer. Then they heard a strange sound from down among the wagons, the sound of an Irish folk song.

Red Cloud looked to Harper. "It is not only us who have medicine this day."

Harper nodded. O'Leary had finally found his way to the gold fields and was playing the same tune he had played along the Platte when he and Harper were returning east and when they had gone to the village to trade with Deals for the boy.

"Maybe it is best if the honor of fighting this day be left to the spirits," Harper suggested.

Red Cloud nodded and looked to Crazy Horse, who also nodded.

"We can find the Bluecoats again another day," Crazy Horse said. "It will be dark soon and the rain is coming heavier. The old Bluecoat had found the medicine of the storm as well and the spirits do not wish us to bother him."

Fox Boy was smiling as Red Cloud and Crazy Horse

turned their ponies back toward the village and were joined by the other warriors. "You will not have to face your friend in battle ever now. He will be gone from this country. But it looks like he is riding one of your ponies."

"We have already met on the field of battle," Harper said. "Once again we traded a life for a horse, as we did in the story I have told you about my trip back to the land of the *Wasicun*. Our lives have crossed in many strange ways."

"Maybe you will see him again," Fox Boy said.

"Maybe. Now let us return to your mother and begin our lives together as a family."

Fox Boy smiled as he washed the paint from his face in the rain. Ahead a singer was making a song of glory for him that would be sung around the village. Harper told Fox Boy his life of honor had begun, as had his own, at a very young age, and together they joined the warriors of Red Cloud and Crazy Horse while behind them through the rain came the sound of a penny whistle.

*If you have enjoyed this book and would like to receive
details of other Walker Western titles,
please write to:*

Westerns Editor
Walker and Company
720 Fifth Avenue
New York, NY 10019